"WHO TOLD YOU HER NAME WAS LUCRECE, STRANGER?"

That seemed to shake old Sextus, too, judging from the way he put down his cup to slither his gun hand out of Longarm's view. Longarm couldn't risk a look-see at the gals off to one side of him. Before the bitty boy could barge in to complicate things even worse, Longarm smiled pleasantly at Uncle Ralph and said, "I never knew this spread was here before. Like yourselves, I spied a distant windmill out in the middle of nowhere. But before I explain further, would both you boys mind reaching for the rafters?"

He saw they did indeed, so he fired under the table first at Uncle Ralph and crabbed sideways from his own chair to blast the so-called Sextus in the lower gut as Uncle Ralph crashed backward to the dirt floor, chair and all.

Both females were screaming fit to bust between the blasts of Longarm's .44-40 as, having started, he thought it best to just finish the sons of bitches off. . . .

TABOR EVANS

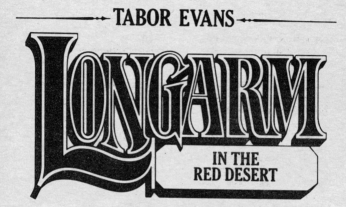

LONGARM

IN THE RED DESERT

J

JOVE BOOKS, NEW YORK

LONGARM IN THE RED DESERT

A Jove Book / published by arrangement with
the author

PRINTING HISTORY
Jove edition / May 1990

ISBN: 0-515-10308-X

PRINTED IN THE UNITED STATES OF AMERICA

10   9   8   7   6   5   4   3   2   1

Chapter 1

The help at the Parthenon Saloon near the Denver Federal Building would have served free firewater to painted and befeathered gents of the sun dance persuasion before they'd have allowed a woman of any race or religion to belly up to the bar in the main taproom.

This was not to say the management held with sissy notions on sobriety, celibacy, or other crimes against nature. In fact, private side rooms were provided where customers of the more delicate sex could get discreetly drunk or downright indelicate, as long as they had sense to keep the infernal doors shut.

U.S. Deputy Marshal Custis Long had not gone over to the Parthenon around noon to get laid though, or even seriously drunk. After a dull morning riding herd on a trio of accused killers in federal court, he was simply hungry as a bitch wolf in the late winter, and, as if to make up for their steep prices on liquid refreshments, the Parthenon served the best free lunch within a day's ride of the office.

So it came to pass that the still fairly young senior deputy of the Denver District Court was innocently inhaling needled beer and pickled pig's feet when a swamper with a tray of empty beer schooners approached to confide, "There's a swell-looking gal around the side as would like a word or more with you, Longarm. Gave her name as Miss Doris Drake. Only she said it wouldn't mean nothing to you."

Longarm washed down a mouthful of free lunch with expensive suds in order to reply in a bemused tone, "She was right. What else might she have looked like, aside from swell?"

The swamper replied wistfully, "Once you've allowed a female's good-looking as well as female, who gives bird turds about details? I think she might have had black hair. I wasn't paying much attention that high up her."

Longarm drained the last of his beer schooner, belched delicately, and asked the helpful swamper for at least a rough estimate of the infernal room number. Then he tipped the son of a bitch, even though he suspected the mysterious Miss Drake had already done so, for all the good it had done either of them.

When he caught up with her in Room B, however, Longarm had to forgive the poor old swamper a mite for describing the pretty little thing so vaguely. "Swell-looking" was the first impression the petite dark beauty made on any man with natural feelings. She rose from the bitty table she'd been seated behind when he stepped in with his hat in his hand and a curious smile on his clean-cut but weather-beaten face. As she held out her own gloved hand for him to shake, kiss, or whatever, he noted her eyes were more a shade of army blue than the black one might have described 'em as being, while her hair was really dark brown instead of ebony. He decided it was her pale skin, almost white as old ivory, that made her hair and eyes look darker than they really were. Her dress, despite its summer weight, was just plain black, as was the fake bird on the straw boater she had pinned atop her upswept hair. It was her own business

2

why she dressed so gloomy. So he just took hold of her black-gloved fingers, gave 'em a friendly shake, and allowed that while he was her servant she seemed to have the advantage on him. When she just went on staring doe eyed at him he added, gallantly but truthfully enough, "Had we ever met before, in peace or war, I'm dead certain I'd have remembered your face and, ah, general appearance, if not the name."

She dimpled demurely and seemed to be hanging on to his fool hand, even though he'd long since let go, as she confided, "We've never met before. But you did meet my baby brother in Durango, just a few months ago, and I'd do anything, anything, to make things right between you, Deputy Long!"

Longarm smiled down at her half mockingly as he replied, "Just my luck I'd get an offer like that whilst I'm pulling court duty. But before you do anything, would you mind informing me what in thunder we might be talking about, ma'am? I'll take your word you have a kid brother you're mighty fond of, but I'll be switched with snakes if I recall anyone named Drake that I've managed to get on the outs with in recent memory, let alone Durango."

She must have wanted to sit down, and since she was hanging on to him for dear life as she did so, they both wound up side by side on the padded bench behind the bitty table. He put his dark brown Stetson down where there was just enough room beside the two tumblers and pint bottle she'd ordered in apparent anticipation. He got out his pocket watch with his free hand as she explained, "They call him Kid Chinks around Durango."

"I got to head back to the Federal Building now, ma'am," Longarm said.

It didn't work. She insisted, "You can't tell me you don't remember him. Everyone says he backed you down in the Chapman Saloon and, what's more, ran you out of town!"

Longarm got his hand back, with some effort, and put his hat back on, saying, "If you say so, ma'am. I do recall

3

a mighty young rascal sporting north-range chinks or knee-length chaps, and I can see how he might have come to such an astounding conclusion. I was in Durango long enough to change trains, as I now recall. The kid had been drinking way too much for a lad his age or any other age, come to study on it. Some other young fool must have told him who I was, or who Ned Buntline and Crawford of the *Denver Post* keep saying I must be, in print.''

He got back to his feet, assuring her, ''There's nothing you ought to worry your pretty little head about, Miss Doris. I wasn't gunning for your kid brother in Durango and I'm surely not gunning for him now.''

She got to her own feet, grabbing for his hand again and winding up with his left sleeve as she almost sobbed, ''I know you took pity on a foolish boy who'd been drinking. Elroy, as we call him in our family, knows this as well.''

Longarm shrugged and said, ''Good for him. I got to get on back to court now, ma'am. It's been nice talking to you about other odd conversations in other saloons, but if it's all the same to you—''

''You can't just dismiss us both!'' she cut in, getting an even better grip on his arm. ''Elroy *called* you, in a whole taproom filled with witnesses! He said right out loud that he didn't think the famous Longarm looked so tough and you, the famous Longarm, *took it* off him, meek as a lamb!''

Longarm grimaced and replied in an injured tone, ''I'd have rather you described me gentle as a calf, ma'am. I had a heap of jobs in my misspent youth but sheepherding wasn't one of 'em.'' Then he tried in vain to twist his fool arm free without any risk of injury to such a delicate-looking little gal as he continued, ''Speaking of jobs, I won't have one with the Justice Department if I don't get it on back to the Federal Building. Judge Palmer has a wicked temper and he's not at all disposed to long lunch breaks when he could just as well be serving out death sentences, and this is about the last day of the trial, they tell me.''

It only worked halfway. The oddly desperate Doris Drake

didn't try to stop him from leaving. She simply refused to let go of his arm as he had to sort of drag her along, muttering, "This is getting sort of silly. For once we get back there I have to fetch the accused up from the holding cells in the cellar and, dang it, no girls are allowed down there, hear?"

She said they'd cross that bridge when they came to it. The walk back to the Federal Building was just long enough for him to get a better grasp on what was eating the poor gal, or, in truth, her dumb kid brother.

Being a grown man, Longarm had felt no call to fire upon or even flatten the flamboyant Kid Chinks just for being an asshole. Since it would have been rude to tell the stubborn little gal her brother was an asshole, he contented himself with explaining, "Nobody with a rep as a gunslick can afford to take up every invite to a gunfight, Miss Doris. As I recall that conversation with the famous Kid Chinks, that dramatic afternoon, he gave me 'til sundown to slap leather or get out of Durango and, seeing as my narrow gauge was leaving no later than four-thirty in any case—"

"You let Elroy run you out of town!" she cut in with a sob.

He could only answer with a dry chuckle, "If that's the way him and his sidekicks saw it, so be it. Like I said, a gent in my line of work can't afford to spend all his waking hours indulged in duels or defending the results of the same in court. I *tried* to tell Ned Buntline that even James Butler Hickok had to fill out depositions in triplicate that time he blew away Dave Tutt in sixty-five to commence his whole pistoliferous career, but, no, old Ned and that infernal Crawford of the *Post* keep describing gunfights as if they were affairs of honor between kids meeting by the swings after school."

"You don't have to convince me how silly the so-called code can get," she said. "I'm sure Elroy would like to take back all those bad names he called you in Durango, now. You see, whether you took that brush with him seriously or not, poor Elroy, as the notorious Kid Chinks, is now known far and wide as the man, indeed the one man, who ever backed the ferocious Longarm down!''

By this time they were crossing over to the Federal Building. So Longarm assured her, ''Aw, I'm not that ferocious and lots of gents have backed me down, if walking away from a pointless argument with a pest can be considered backing down. I can't take you down to the holding cells with me, ma'am, so if you'd be kind enough to unhold my arm—''

''They're going to kill him!'' she cut in, clinging even tighter to his arm as he managed, even so, to get them both across the street without getting kicked by a horse or kicking up any freshly dropped horse droppings. He didn't want to know who ''they'' were, but she insisted on telling him, anyway. She said, ''Since he's become known as the shootist even shootists like Longarm are afraid of, he's been called by more than one young gent of like persuasion, who'd like to be known as the man who backed down, or beat, the man who backed down you know who!''

Longarm rolled his eyes heavenward and muttered, ''Why me, Lord? I didn't even need that flat warm beer that time in Durango!'' Then he told her, or tried to, ''There's nothing I can do about your kid brother's problem, ma'am. Nothing I'd want to do, at any rate. Even if I was willing to go back for a rematch, I fail to see how anything either of us could do or say would change the past. If I let him shoot me, or even back me down some more, it would only add to his fame and hence his problem. I assume you're not asking that I shoot him and just get it over with?''

Before she could answer, Deputy Guilfoyle came partway down the granite steps to wave them up his way. Longarm was game. He and the gal in black joined the gray-suited Guilfoyle on the steps, and Longarm introduced them tersely and told his fellow deputy he had to go down to the cellar for ''those rascals Judge Palmer aims to string up.''

Guilfoyle shook his head and replied, ''Not hardly, Longarm. I was on my way to the Parthenon for our boss when I spied you and this prettier critter coming. Marshal Vail just put Smiley and Dutch in our places in Palmer's court. Don't ask me what I'm supposed to do the rest of this sunny day and I won't mention it either. They just told me to fetch you for old Billy Vail, and now that I've done so, what's on the free-lunch counter at the Parthenon?''

Longarm said his fellow deputy would find the usual boiled eggs and pickled pig's feet if he hurried, since they both went fast and tended to be replaced by two varieties of cheese, both stale. Then, since Doris Drake was still clinging to him, demanding he do something about her demented brother, he just trudged on up to the second floor and into the office suite of Marshal William Vail of the Denver District Court, Federal, in hopes she'd either let go or say something more sensible. She was doing neither as old Henry, the skinny young squirt who played the type-writer out front, glanced up, stared more owlishly than usual, and murmured, ''The marshal said to send you right back to him the moment you arrived and, ah, might this young lady be with you?''

Longarm shot him a disgusted look and said, ''Anyone can see she ain't with *you,* Henry.'' But as he tried once more to disengage his arm he saw it was likely to cause as much of a fuss either way. So he just shrugged and sashayed back to Billy Vail's oak-paneled inner sanctum with the fool gal clinging to him like a silly but sort of seductive limpit.

He naturally wasn't nearly as surprised to see her in Billy Vail's office as Billy Vail seemed to be. As his older, stubbier, cigar-chomping superior rose gallantly behind his cluttered desk at the sight of such an unexpected pleasure, as he put it, Longarm told her she could sit in the one decent chair on their side of the desk if she was about ready to let go of his arm, now.

She sobbed, ''You can't just abandon me in this fix, sir!''

Billy Vail cocked one suspicious eyebrow at them both and growled, ''Dad blast it, Longarm, I've warned you not to mix your duties to this office with your, ah, social affairs, and having it out with a woman scorned in my very office is, to put it mildly—"

"Hold your fire, boss!" Longarm cut in with an expression of sincere innocence. "Miss Doris and I have never done anything half as social as you seem to be intimating, and you ought to be ashamed of yourself. She's just fussing at me because I had a chance to pistolwhip her kid brother a few months ago and passed on the opportunity."

Vail allowed that made even less sense than his own first thoughts on the subject. So Longarm let the gal explain about her fool brother. Vail let out a low mournsome whistle and told her, "You're right, ma'am. My heart bleeds for you and young Elroy, only I can't see a way to get him off the hook he put himself on, no offense."

She said, "If only Custis would come back to Durango with me, so that everyone could see him, well, pistolwhip silly Elroy like he said he could have."

The two grown men in the room exchanged glances. Longarm had been staring longer at the way she bulged that black poplin from inside. He still considered how far off and tedious Durango was as he shrugged and said, "I reckon I could get down to that corner of Colorado and back over the weekend, if I put my mind to it, boss."

Vail brushed the front of that black summer-weight dress with his own knowing eyes as he muttered, "I know all too well how long it might take you, once you've put your mind, or any other parts, to anything this office has no call to mess with. But that's neither here nor there. I never took you off that court duty to send you down to Durango. I just got an urgent request by wire from the BLM."

Vail noticed how his uninvited female guest was gaping at him, so he politely explained, "Bureau of Land Management, Interior Department, ma'am. I fear Longarm has more serious duties to the taxpayers than to any would-be Wild Bill who should have known better."

Ignoring the protests he'd evoked by saying that, Billy

8

Vail went on to tell Longarm, "I've got to send you up to the Red Desert of Wyoming to serve a writ on a would-be sheep baron who keeps scaring range-fee collectors from the BLM. You know the place so well by now and—"

"Hold on and back up a mite!" Longarm cut in. "Just where on any map would you want to place such an oddly designated stretch of Wyoming, boss?"

Vail shrugged and decided, "The middle of Mongolia sounds like as good a place as any, if it was up to me alone. The boys who drew up the survey maps for Interior must have been the ones who decided to call that confusion of rimrock and sage flats between the Wind River and Sierra Madre ranges a red desert. Suffice it to say we've had you up yonder often enough after everything from Shoshone to train robbers and—"

"I wish you'd send one of the other boys out on this one, Uncle Billy," Longarm cut in, causing Billy Vail to gape at him owl eyed and slack jawed all the time it took Longarm to gently but firmly sit Doris Drake in the guest chair and perch himself on the arm of the same, since she just wouldn't let go.

Vail recovered his composure as well as the unlit cigar he'd allowed to drop from his gaping mouth to his cluttered desk and decided, "You surely have an odd sense of humor, old son. I'm sure I'd get your dry jokes if there was anything at all funny about the remarks you pass while I'm trying to give you serious instructions."

The brunette clinging so stubbornly to Longarm's arm all this time pouted, "You just can't send Custis off to any old Red Desert now that I've tracked him down at last."

Vail sighed and said, "Sure I can. I have to. The BLM is banking on us to enforce some federal law in uncertain country Longarm is more certain of than any other white man on our payroll at the moment."

Longarm shook his head and said, "I don't want the chore. Don't they still have a federal marshal in Cheyenne, and ain't Cheyenne closer to the country in question?"

Vail nodded but said, "The Cheyenne office ain't that much closer and, even if they were, they have enough on their plate this summer, thanks to some serious discussion of fence lines and water rights in other parts of a mighty disorganized as well as oversized territory."

Vail struck a match on the edge of his desk to relight his evil-smelling cigar stub before he explained, "We've no jurisdictional dispute with any other lawmen up that way, Longarm. I got the writ they want you to serve out front, along with the travel orders old Henry's typing up for you. I'll allow it could be a hard row to hoe for a greenhorn who didn't know the high country. But serving a simple writ on a stockman who can't know the country half as well as any Shoshone ought to be duck soup for a man who knows his way about up yonder the way you do!"

Longarm didn't answer. Vail insisted, "Staring stubborn don't cut no ice with this child, Longarm. If you have a halfway sensible reason to be excused from this detail, spit it out."

Longarm couldn't. He wasn't a kiss-and-tell type to begin with, and if he had been it might have sounded like bragging to go on about that beautiful young blonde up by Bitter Creek with a beautiful brunette from Durango hanging on to every word as well as his poor arm.

Vail said, more soothingly, "You told us you'd made a heap of friends up yonder the time we sent you after Cotton Younger. So what have you got to worry about in them parts, old son?"

Longarm sighed and said, "Let me do the worrying. Like you just said, the chore don't sound half as complicated as the wide-open high range itself. So with any luck I might not run into anyone more murderous than the cuss they want me to serve with them pesky legal papers."

There were times it seemed all the ladies Longarm knew in both Denver and the biblical sense managed to get sore at him at the same time. So for this reason, and the simple fact that a man had to have some damned place to store his more serious possibles, Longarm had long kept his own furnished digs at a rooming house on the unfashionable side of Cherry Creek.

As a rule he only had to change his duds and pick up his personal saddle and such before he was free to head out into the field, set for come what may. And as a rule he didn't have an infernal female clinging to his now-numb arm as he slogged across the sand banks of the creek at low water and along the cinder-paved path to the rooming house in question. As he spied the lace curtains of his sometimes less than understanding landlady ahead of them, now, he told the persistent pretty pest, "Yonder's where you're just going to have to let go long enough for me to change out of this sissy tweed suit and strap some possibles to my old McClellan, Miss Doris. I'm sure you'll find it more comfortable in the downstairs parlor if I can't talk you into waiting on the porch."

She protested, "How do I know you won't duck out the back way and escape to that vast Red Desert, Custis?"

He laughed despite himself and assured her, "I told you it was a free country when I told you where I was headed, next, on government business. I don't have to climb no backyard fences with a saddle and saddle gun on my fool back when the time must come for us to part."

As they swung into the dooryard toward the somewhat worn but recently swept front steps of his house-proud landlady, Longarm said, "It'd take me far too long to get up to Wyoming Territory aboard real horse flesh. So I mean to catch the iron horse north to Cheyenne and change to the westbound U.P. as far as Thayer Junction before I hire me a real horse to track down that sheep baron."

As he helped her up the steps he added, "The reason I'm telling you all this is to avoid more confusion once we finally get over to the railroad yards this afternoon. I'm catching a Burlington freight train north, while you'll want to board

11

the Denver and Rio Grande Western for Durango, of course.''

There was nobody lurking in the hall when he sort of dragged her in there with him, having little choice in the matter. He still wished she'd keep her voice down, or at least less strident, when she sobbed, ''I won't go back to Durango without you! You can't make me! We have to save Elroy, you brute!''

Longarm sighed and led the way into the front parlor. He was glad to see it was empty. He didn't know where his landlady might be at the moment, but naturally the other boarders were still at work at this time of the day. He tried to get Doris to sit some damned place, and when that didn't work he told her, on the stairs as they both seemed headed for his digs up yonder, ''This is getting downright awkward, no offense. I just told you I meant to change my pants upstairs, and even if I wasn't my landlady would have a fit if she knew I was sneaking gals up to my room, unchaperoned.''

Doris gave his numb arm an almost playful squeeze and answered, ''Pooh, we're not doing anything sneaky. Leave the hall door open if you're afraid someone might think I'm out to get fresh with you in your room!''

He laughed. For he could see before they got there that like a lot of plans laid by mice and men, that one was doomed by the simple fact it was more embarrassing to change one's duds with the hall door wide agape than in front of an uninvited guest, of either sex. So once they were up in his corner digs he not only shut the door but bolted it on the inside and, when she asked him in a suspicious tone just how she was supposed to take that, he told her, ''Take a walk around the block or all the way home for that matter. I never invited you up here, with any intent at all, but since nobody else would buy that, I'd as soon not advertise your presence. So present yourself down on yonder bed or window seat and try to stay out of my way just a few cotton-picking minutes, hear?''

She sat on the bed, bouncing the springs experimentally like a sassy girl-child as he tried not to laugh. It wasn't the way she looked atop the covers, even bouncing, in her sober summer dress. It was the way she was reminding him of how he'd come by those new and almost silent bedsprings. He'd been certain the landlady would evict him that time he'd busted the old springs with the help of a fleshy as well as frisky Mexican gal whose name escaped him at the moment.

First things coming first Longarm stood with his back to his somewhat less buxom guest, facing the mirror above his battered dresser as he emptied out his pockets and removed his hat and guns, including the wicked little derringer attached to one end of an innocent-looking watch chain. He checked the chambers of his double-action. 44-40 as well, even though he'd gone through all these same fool motions that very morning. There was nothing foolish about making sure one's guns and billfold were loaded, even when one wasn't planning on field duty in tedious country. He made sure he had plenty of waterproof matches to go with his cheroots, noted he'd best pick up more cheroots in Cheyenne, and glanced in the mirror at the perky brunette on his bed to warn, ''Stare out the rear window if you shock easy, ma'am. I mean to change into clean underwear as well as duds more suited to range riding in high summer.''

She didn't seem to care what might be out back. So, having done his duty by her and not really half as shy about his own bare ass as old Queen Victoria seemed to feel he ought to be, Longarm proceeded to get undressed. He was only halfway naked when she told him she could see why everyone was so scared of him. She said, ''My heavens, you sure do seem to have a lot of muscles, Custis.''

He grunted, ''You ain't seen half the bulges I'm capable

13

of. But you surely might, if you don't cease and desist further flirtatious comments on my figure.''

She dimpled up at him to ask, demurely, ''Will you come with me if I let you, ah, bulge all you want, Custis?''

He laughed incredulously and said, ''If you're talking about my coming with you to Durango you know I can't, much as I might like to come with you more ways than I dare mention.''

She sighed and reached absently behind her with both hands as she said, ''I guess you just didn't believe me when I said I'd do anything, anything you wanted, if only you'd help out my poor baby brother.''

As he stood there in his underdrawers and socks, listening to her unsnap the back of her black dress, he just hated to hear himself saying, as he knew he had to, ''Hold on, now, honey! This has gotten past fooling around into cruelty to animals!''

It got crueler, in a sort of humorous way, when she stood up to let her unhooked dress cascade down around her high-buttoned ankles, facing him in only her black stockings and straw hat, to demand, ''Do you still think you can run off to the Red Desert without me?''

He stepped closer, taking her nude charms firmly in hand as she in turn unbuttoned his underdrawers to handle him as well, asking, dreamy eyed, ''Heavens, is all this meant for little old me?''

He lowered both their bare bodies to the bed covers, but told her even as she welcomed him with loving arms and wide-spread thighs, ''You heard my boss order me up to Wyoming Territory. But I might be willing to meet you halfway.''

She gasped, ''Oh, Lordy, I'm sure that's in more than halfway, and don't hesitate on my account, darling!''

He felt he had to. He eased into her all the way, as any mortal man would have felt obliged to, but he murmured in one shell-like ear, as she dug her nails into his bare buttocks, ''You can tag along with me to Wyoming Territory

14

if you've a mind to. It may serve to keep us both out of trouble until I do have the time to carry you back to Durango and get things straight with the rest of your family. Do we have a deal?''

She said they surely did and proved it by taking off her dumb hat and getting on top. Before they calmed down enough to share a smoke and some pillow planning he was certainly glad he'd paid his outraged landlady the price of these new bedsprings. For even though Doris seemed way skinnier than that chunky Mex gal, they'd have surely busted any bedsprings the least bit worn.

He was sure the whole damned household knew what they were up to up here behind closed doors by the time the two of them were taking turns on a cheroot with the late-afternoon sun painting pretty patterns of sunlight and shade on their bare and barely sated flesh. For it was after quitting time and here and there a door slammed or footsteps thudded elsewhere in the house. Naturally Doris, having just about raped Longarm in his own bed, asked nervously, *now*, what the odds on anyone walking in on them might be.

He assured her, ''Nobody's apt to. The other boarders know I keep heaps of guns and ammunition up here. If we're going to have this sweet little ass of yours along on the Red Desert, we're going to have to get you a saddle and some sensible duds to cover it. Let's see, now . . . It's too late to outfit you at Muller's or the Denver Dry Goods. On the other hand, we might get a better price on better gear if we just wait until we reach Cheyenne and pick you up some new duds and a used saddle. I hope you know how to ride astride and handle a saddle gun, honey.''

She gulped and asked, ''Heavens, didn't Marshal Vail just order you to ride out to some sheep spread and serve some legal papers on its owner?''

Longarm took a drag on the cheroot and placed it between her lusher lips as he told her, ''He did. I may have paid more attention to the written complaint from Land Man-

15

agement. They've tried to serve him at his officious home address on their homestead charts as to exact longitude and latitude. The cuss seems to spend an awesome amount of time out on open range, with his sheep and work crews. I know it sounds dumb, but you can't get a judgment in court on anyone, for anything, unless you can somehow manage to serve him with a written invite to said court. The writ they want me to serve him with, and swear under oath I did it, is a lot less complicated than the range hog's current whereabouts. It's just a notice warning him to cease and desist from grazing his stock on public land or show cause in court why he ought to go on feeding his fool sheep on Uncle Sam.''

She handed back the smoke to say with one of those soft sighs bored females are prone to heave, ''I don't see what good I'd be to you riding astride with, good Lord, a repeating rifle? What if I were to just wait for you in town while you tracked down your mysterious sheepherder, darling?''

He gripped the cheroot between his teeth and bounced her unbound hair some as he shrugged his broad bare shoulders, saying, ''We'd both no doubt wind up sort of lonesome after sundown. Billy Vail wouldn't be sending me up yonder to serve a writ if he expected the confounded sneak to leave a clear and easy trail. We're talking unfenced open range like a mighty wrinkled rug for eighty-odd miles by over a hundred, or, in sum, eight or nine thousand square miles to cover, which no one lawman could. I did some scouting up around the South Pass for the army when the Shoshone rose in seventy-eight, and to tell the truth, whole war bands managed to hide from me amidst all that sage and rimrock.''

She propped herself up on one naked arm to demand, ''Good grief, how long do you expect me to wait for you to finish serving the silly man his silly writ so we can get on down to Durango?''

He shrugged again and said he didn't know, adding, ''If

Billy Vail's told the BLM we'll do it, I reckon he expects me to do it, even if it takes all summer. I never said just when we might ever get you back to Durango, you know. You can start for there now, if my company is already getting tedious to you.''

She must not have been ready to leave, judging from all the effort she put into coming some more with him that same afternoon.

Chapter 2

Longarm was neither rude enough to ask a lady to hop a freight with him nor rich enough to spring for the private compartment Doris asked about when they boarded the Burlington Night Flyer bound for Cheyenne. She took riding upright in a coach seat like a good sport, and he made it up to her by hiring them a room with a bath, or at least a sink and crapper, when they checked into the Hotel Victoria across from the Cheyenne depot before midnight. They even managed to get some sleep before the hustle and bustle of the big city inspired Longarm to tear off a morning quickie, a washup, and those courtesy calls a lawman was required to make in another lawman's territory, if he knew what was good for him.

Leaving Doris slugabed with her long dark hair unbound and her welcome mat still hot for him, she said, Longarm fed his own face downstairs and paid room service to tote more sausages and flapjacks up to any pretty lady they might find in Room 306 before he mosied out into the bright morning sunlight to get his bearings as he lit a cheroot. He'd been to the Federal Building in Cheyenne before. So he headed for there first. Cheyenne had its main streets paved, now, but there was still a more rawboned look to the place than downtown Denver could brag of this late in the nineteenth century, so nobody shot snooty looks his way as he passed 'em wearing his cross-draw rig wide open on a denim-clad hip with neither a sissy frock coat nor that son-of-a-bitching shoestring tie they expected a government employee of his status to sport since President Hayes and Miss Lemonade Lucy had been running the country and dictating current fashion. As he passed a saddle shop Longarm made a mental note about the less fashionable duds and other trail gear he still had to pick up for good old Doris. They'd naturally brought along her own traveling bags, but as he'd suspected even before he'd ridden her, she hadn't come up from Durango with much riding in mind. Not much pony riding, at any rate. It wouldn't have been delicate to ask a lady he'd just met up with who she might have had in mind when she'd packed all those items of feminine hygene in her carpetbag before leaving Durango. He knew he ought to be glad she had. He wondered why it was that love-'em-and-leave-'em rascals like himself had to feel sort of shortchanged every time they met up with the kind of gal they all said they were just dying to meet.

He told himself, for maybe the hundredth time since he'd met up with her, that the beautiful but neither too brilliant nor bashful brunette had been just what the doctor ordered for another chore up this way. For they weren't anywhere near the home spread of the rich young Widow Stover, yet, and he was already fighting the infernal temptation. He kept telling himself there was simply nothing Kim Stover could do for him with her beautiful blonde body that good old Doris couldn't manage as well, or, hell, almost as well. That certain magic only one couple out of a hundred or more ever fell under in the same bed was another of those mysteries a gent in his line of work couldn't afford to dwell upon.

Money being no object to gents who got to spend the more honestly gotten gains of the taxpaying public, the Federal Building up in Cheyenne was about as grand as the one in Denver, despite the old Indian woman selling baskets on the front steps. Billy Vail's opposite number in Wyoming Territory was too grand to invite a mere deputy back to his own inner sanctum. But their own version of Henry, albeit somewhat older and gruffer, climbed out from behind his own typewriter to open a filing cabinet, haul out a pint of Kentucky mash, and treat Longarm right as they agreed on the terms of his expedition to the Red Desert.

They were too busy to give rabbit squat about sheep accused of stealing sagebrush a good two hundred miles away in a territory way too big for the manpower on hand, federal, territorial, or domestic. As the Cheyenne clerk refilled his visitor's tin cup he explained, "The land office has pestered us about the case, of course. So I can tell you one of their own dudes rode out of Honeycomb to serve that cease and desist on old L. J. Travis about a month back. I'll allow it seems a mite suspicious that nobody ever saw hide nor hair of the sissy since, but I ask you, would it be fair or at all pragmatic to charge Travis and his all-too-many sheepherders with whatever in thunder really happened to the cuss?"

Longarm squinted his gray eyes to picture his mental map of the area, such as it was, as he mused half to himself, "The town of Honeycomb would be near the north end of the trail between Atlantic City and Thayer Junction, right?"

"Yep. Ain't no railroad in them parts, yet. They do say L. J. Travis ships his mutton out of Thayer Junction on Bitter Creek. But he grazes the stupid stinky critters up around the aprons of the Wind River foothills, where the range gets a mite more summer rain."

Longarm nodded soberly and allowed he knew the sort of bumpy open range they were talking about, adding,

"Billy Vail gave me the facts and figures down Denver way. I figure to get more detailed directions to the Travis home spread once I swap a railroad seat for a cow pony in Thayer Junction. I've, ah, ridden that trail north a time or two in the past."

The man who kept records for the Cheyenne office brightened and agreed, "By jimmies, so you have! We're still laughing about the time you stole a prisoner out from under that Canadian Mountie up in the Wind River range. Didn't you ride with the young Widow Stover and her boys against some other pests up in them parts?"

Longarm looked away as he muttered, "Same pests. A master of disguise had a heap of lawmen from both sides of the border sort of confused. This case I'm working on now couldn't hold much interest to Kim Stover and her riders, she and them being more concerned with cows than wooly backed coyote bait."

The Wyoming gent nodded soberly and declared, "I agree neither our good Lord nor Wakan Tonka ever intended all that high-country sage for fucking *sheep*! The reason I brung up local cattle folk was that you could doubtless trust 'em better when it comes to seeking missing government men on range all shit-up by sheep. The BLM tells us the stockmen grazing cows in and about the Red Desert have been reasonable about their grazing fees since the Red Sash Gang's been acting up. I reckon they figure an accurate tally for their theft insurance policies beats shaving the grazing fees by forgetting just how much stock they might have to lose for real."

Longarm finished the contents of his cup but held on to it to keep the clerk from refilling it this early in the day. He said, "The Stover herds would be grazing way up the west slopes of the Wind Rivers, this time of the year." Then something the Wyoming man had said sank deeper and Longarm cocked an eyebrow to demand, "Hold on. Did you just tell me some total asshole's been trying to

peddle insurance policies on the lives and probable whereabouts of Wyoming *cows*?''

The clerk poured himself another drink as he nodded soberly as ever and replied, ''Asshole or not, he's insured a
heap of stock of late, thanks to the Red Sash Gang. The premiums run about a dime a head as long as you're willing to
insure at least a thousand of the same. If they wind up lost,
strayed or stolen the policy pays off ten dollars a head.''

Longarm nodded in a noncommittal manner as he politely
placed the tin cup on one corner of the filing cabinet. He
hadn't been sent all this way to set a fair price on Wyoming
beef and it was rude to sass one's elders. So instead of
saying the Red Sash Gang was a myth on a par with the
sinister Side Hill Snorter, he just said he had to touch base
with the BLM office here in town, wherever in thunder it
might be.

The clerk in the marshal's office informed Longarm he
was in luck. For the Cheyenne branch of the federal land
office was just down the hall, and he could make it before
they knocked off for noon dinner if he started out about
now. So they shook on that and parted friendly.

The long marble corridor seemed empty for the hour and
dimly lit for how brightly the sun was glaring from a cloudless sky outside. As Longarm strode toward the big but sort
of soot-grimed window at one far end he decided it was the
contrast between daylight, even sooty daylight, and the dark
shades of shiny rock the architect had favored once they'd
told him money was no object. The well-named Rocky
Mountains grew rocks of all kinds and colors save white
marble. So the floor slabs were a sort of rusty red while the
walls on either side of him looked more like petrified and
polished bacon, fried, except where oak doors gleaming
under orange shellac broke the more expensive surface. He
noticed the rooms were odd numbered along the wall he
was striding closer to. He knew the land office was numbered 206. So as he hauled even with 205 to his left he
spun gracefully on one heel to cut right and, as he did so,

23

a six-gun roared behind him, something buzzed close enough to the nape of his neck to set all the hairs there atingle, glass shattered down at the far end of the hall, and Longarm was flat on his gut, facing the blue haze of gunsmoke down the other way with his own gun drawn, all at about the same time.

Nobody seemed to be there, at first. Then, just as Longarm was fixing to fire into all that blue gunsmoke for luck, the infernal hall filled up with screaming men and cussing women from the offices on both damned sides.

As Longarm got wearily back to his feet some asshole with a badge pinned to his buckskin vest yelled, "Drop that gun!" at him, even though anyone could see he was putting the damned .44-40 back in its holster, unfired.

Then the clerk he'd just been jawing with in the marshal's office called out, "It's all right, Matt. He's one of our own, from the Denver office."

So nobody got to shoot anybody, now that the noisy back-shooting son of a bitch who'd busted the window seemed long gone. But Longarm got to say more about him than he really knew. Once he'd tersely denied shooting at yonder window with his own pistol he could only add, "Now you boys know as much as I do. I never laid eye-one on the sneaky rascal. It appears he was already crawfishing for the nearest stairwell when he pegged that one shot at me. His aim was a mite high but accurate enough, had I not made a sudden turn he just couldn't have expected."

The one in the buckskin vest, who must have read the sort of magazines that showed such costumes on their covers at this late date, said, "He must have been expecting you to show up here at this very address this very morning, Deputy Long. If you're the Denver deputy they call Longarm one can see why he didn't see fit to hang about and explain things to you, once he saw he'd missed!"

Longarm could only shrug modestly. He felt even dumber when a pleasingly plump stenographer gal in the crowd asked what a Longarm might be, and a squirt with pencils stuck behind both ears told her knowingly, "The closest thing to the Black Plague on the federal payroll. You back-shoot a lawman like Longarm stone dead with your first shot or you don't shoot at all. For they say few men have yet to get off a second shot, after missing him with their first one!"

Longarm couldn't look at the gal after that. The clerk who seemed to know so much about the Red Sash Gang opined, "Some outlaws must have been expecting this visit, Longarm."

Longarm replied with a dubious snort, "I never told one soul I was coming to this particular address this morning. So how do you like someone following me here?"

The lawman in the buckskin vest decided, "It works if we assume the would-be assassin was holding his fire for a crack at you in front of no witnesses."

Longarm nodded soberly and said, "That's the way he had me, up until a few moments ago. Has anyone here ever considered how handy it would be to have eyes in the back of one's head as well as a badge to tote through such an unfriendly world?"

By this time a more important cheese, attracted by all the commotion out in the hall, had drifted grandly through the crowd to ask the clerk what on earth was going on out here. Longarm didn't have to ask who he was when his clerk explained, "The Red Sash Gang just tried to back-shoot this here Denver boy I told you about, Marshal."

The Cheyenne office's answer to Billy Vail favored Longarm with an annoyed glance of dismissal and muttered, "Nonsense. The Red Sash Gang is just a tall tale made up to green the greenhorns. I can smell the gunsmoke. That's not saying anything important happened out here. I don't know what it is about government offices that draws so many drunks and lunatics."

Longarm smiled thinly and said, "Takes one to know one, Marshal. But, for the record and lest you get me in trouble with my own office, be it known and hereby recorded

I'm standing here cold sober with five rounds in the wheel of my unfired side arm.''

The Cheyenne marshal wrinkled his nose and said, ''I can smell just how sober you might be from here. I'll take your word it was somebody else discharging firearms out here, and unless one or more of you know just who gets to pay for yonder window, we'd best all get back to work, hear?''

That sounded as fair to Longarm as any of the other surly noises coming from the crowd in the crowded corridor. So he nodded and moved across to the land office he'd been headed for in the first place. There didn't seem to be anyone in the reception room until the pleasingly plump gal who'd asked about him outside followed him inside to ask if there was any way she could be of service to him.

He doubted she meant that the way it could be taken. So he told her he was packing a writ for her outfit and explained his need for further helpful hints, adding, ''I got the Travis spread located within a mile or so of that quarter section old Travis laid first claim to, ma'am. But since he never seems to be home to process servers, I'd like to know more about the open range he's been overstocking, to hear you tell it.''

The plump receptionist moved around to her side of the desk in the center of the room as she denied ever telling anyone a thing about anyone called Travis. She added that her boss and his private secretary had left for lunch, if not the day. When Longarm asked if the missing secretary was as pretty as she was the plump gal blushed and flustered, ''Prettier. I can see you're a man of the world, Deputy Long, so do I really have to explain why there's just no saying when or even if they might be back this afternoon?''

He sighed and said, ''I'm commencing to see why the Interior Department borrowed me all the way up from Denver. I can't work up much excitement over a mutton mogul possibly pilfering sagebrush on marginal range, either. But someone in Interior must have noticed my own boss, Billy

26

Vail, takes government business serious. So as long as I'm here I'd best go through anything you have on file about old L. J. Travis. Where might I find such files, in the back?"

The plump receptionist had just nestled her ample behind behind her desk, but she sprang back to her feet with amazing grace as Longarm moved toward the doorway she must have been ordered to defend with her life. She told him, "You can't go in the back without permission, sir!"

So he demanded, "Give me some permission, then. Ain't you in command of this post with everyone else somewhere else in the pursuit of happiness?"

She told him with a blush and bitter smile it seemed a mite unfair to her as well, but added, "I know we both work for the same government, and I'm sure M. Corrigan would be proud to open any and all files to you. But I don't have the authority and, even if I did, I don't have a key to the file room."

Longarm reached thoughtfully in his pants for his all-purpose pocketknife as he suggested with a smile, "Let's eat this apple one bite at a time, Miss, ah . . . ?"

"Daisy, Daisy Brooks," she replied demurely, before asking him how apples had gotten into this conversation.

He got out his knife and unfolded one sort of sneaky blade as he explained, "You can only take one bite out of an apple at a time and you can only argue with a woman point by point. So before we fuss about whether I can get into them files, don't you reckon we ought to find out whether I can get into the file room?"

She insisted, "It's locked. To save locking up each filing cabinet at quitting time, Mr. Corrigan keeps all of them behind one locked door and I just don't have a key to it, see?"

Longarm held up the serrated knife blade, saying, "I might. It's a good thing I pack a badge as well as burglar tools. Would you like to be a sport about showing me which lock I got to pick first, Miss Daisy?"

She hesitated, then she told her missing boss, "Well,

27

Mr. Corrigan, he was packing a gun and I knew you wouldn't want him getting into you liquor cabinet whilst you were out.'' Then she led the way back with an arch smile over one shoulder.

The narrow door set between the big shot's inner office and the cubbyhole his secretary typed in was solid oak with serious brass hardware. So it took Longarm almost a full minute to tinker the heavy lock open. Daisy still clapped her hands in delight and said he was ever so clever as she followed him inside.

There wasn't all that much of an inside to stand in, what with shoulder-high filing cabinets jammed cheek by jowl, even under the one small window. Daisy bumped the door shut after them with her ample hips. That gave them a mite more space to stand in. She said she refused to be held responsible for anything else that might occur in here while her boss was out of the office, and added that she didn't know just what he was looking for to begin with.

He put his knife away, hitched his gun rig to rest his .44-40 a mite forward for a quick draw but less awkward for moving about in such confined spaces, and proceeded to do his own scouting through the files.

They were naturally kept cross indexed in alphabetical order. So it didn't take him long to determine L. J. Travis of Honeycomb Township between the Antelope Hills and Tanglewaters had indeed made a deal to graze nineteen hundred head of sheep on or about the public lands known as the Red Desert, Great Divide Basin, or South Pass Country, depending on just whose survey map one was looking at. The BLM tended to think of it as desert because that was what it sure acted like when one tried to homestead on it. The railroaders, since they owned a heap of track-side sections they'd just love to sell off to some would-be farm folk, naturally liked to think of the area as a big old basin, which sounded a heap wetter than Red Desert. The army had told Longarm he was scouting the South Pass Country for them that time because the only importance the army attached to all that open country was the handy route if afforded mounted war parties, headed either way over the otherwise awkward Continental Divide. When Wakan Tonka had created the Shining Mountains with the help of First Bear they'd somehow neglected to connect up the Wind River peaks with the jagged-ass Sierra Madre eighty-odd miles to the south. The really sneaky part, which was easy to miss sitting down in a train or on a pony in clement weather, was that you were still way the hell up along the Great Divide no matter what you called the confusing miles of gently rolling open range. Grazing fees were low as the BLM set 'em, up yonder, for the simple reason that the grazing was poor, the night winds were cruel, and if wolves and worse didn't take your stock a blizzard could wipe 'em all out as late as June or early as September. Just the same, Longarm had to agree it hardly seemed right to pay the modest grazing fees on nineteen hundred head if one was selling off twice that many spring lambs a year. He told Daisy, "I've always figured we have so many illiterates in Leavenworth because you have to know how to read before you can see what a clear trail you could be leaving on paper. My boss, Billy Vail, is the real caution at this kind of work. But even I can see there's just no way nineteen hundred sheep at their most passionate could lamb three to five thousand times per annum, and it says here he's been selling breeding stock and mutton as well!"

"Then you've found all you wanted back here?" she asked with a sort of wistful sigh.

He shook his head ruefully and told her, "Not hardly. There's nothing on paper saying just where on a mess of open range old L.J. might range most of his sheep. They might know at your branch office in Honeycomb, of course. Meanwhile I'd best put this folder away."

He meant it and he would have had she not made her own awkward attempt to help and wound up hindering considerable. She was too pretty and flustered to outright cuss at, but Longarm still muttered about lard asses and butterfingers inside his head as he hunkered down to gather the papers scattered on the floor all around their feet. He hissed, "Stay put! Don't stampede across this mess!" as she planted the sole of one high-button shoe smack in the center of a range inspector's report. Before she could damage the onionskin paper further Longarm grabbed her ankle to sort of lift her foot from the paper. Her fool ankle was downright armored in patent leather, but to hear her tell it he'd just shoved a hand up her dress to home plate. For the next thing he knew she'd leaped halfway to the ceiling to come down atop him in a soft perfumed pile, and he had to laugh as he considered how dumb they'd look to anyone else, had anyone else been in there with them.

But there wasn't, even if there'd been room, and as he helped her sit up, at least, he recalled how that door opened and shut on a snap lock. So he kissed her and said, "Long as we're both down this way, we'd best gather up these fool papers before we tear 'em up even worse."

She didn't reply in words but got right to work on her hands and knees, blushing fit to bust. They naturally bumped elbows and other parts a mite as they gathered all the scattered papers together, and even Longarm was feeling a mite blushful by the time they had the folder back in alphabetical if not apple-pie order. Gripping it tightly lest they have to go through all that again, Longarm helped Daisy to her feet with his free hand, placing the folder atop the file cabinet behind her instead of in the drawer she had her ample derriere pressed against. She asked him, sort of wet eyed, how come he'd kissed her, down yonder. He chuckled fondly and confided, "I don't know you well enough to kiss you down yonder. I reckon I kissed your lips, in a sort of brotherly way, because you looked so confounded and in need of some comforting."

She lowered her lashes and murmured, "Oh, I thought it was because you found me attractive. I guess you feel I'm too fat for a Don Johnny with your rep, huh? I've heard the tale they tell about you and that French bawd, Sarah Bernhardt.''

Longarm shook his head and said, ''You heard wrong, Miss Daisy. To begin with the lady you just mean-mouthed is a national treasure of France, not no bawd. I was only assigned to bodyguard her when she toured our West that time. We got along all right and I'd be lying if I said I didn't think she looked swell in tights. But the only time I ever kissed her it was just as brotherly.''

''Show me how you kissed Sarah Bernhardt,'' Daisy Brooks said with mighty interesting smoke signals rising in her amber eyes. So he kissed her again, brotherly, and when that felt so good he kissed her the way she'd likely expected him to kiss a French lady, judging by what she was doing with her own passionate tongue.

She didn't seem to care how she got kissed until he had her underdrawers down around her ankles, but even as she stepped out of them she pleaded, ''Not on that dirty floor again, darling. Can't we wait until I get off this afternoon?''

He didn't think she wanted to hear about a slimmer brunette who'd already be wondering where in thunder he'd run off to. So he allowed Daisy to think it was pure passion when he slid open a drawer to either side of her, gripped both with her plump legs hooked over his forearms, and proceeded to do what just about any man might have done in such an inviting albeit somewhat awkward position.

As he entered her, the grips of his six-gun teasing her as well, she giggled, and he was sort of glad he'd torn off that morning quickie back at the hotel. For Daisy was mighty firmly and powerfully built, where it really counted, and he'd have never been able to last long enough to please them both with his first discharge, had he been starting fresh with anyone this sweetly enthusiastic.

As she shuddered in passion on his shaft and asked, ''More?'' in a tone of delight, Longarm wasn't sure he was being as kind to himself as she seemed to think he was being to her. He'd never figured out why meeting up with willing women seemed such an all-or-nothing proposition. He simply knew that if he hadn't had a sure lay waiting for him back at the hotel, this randy receptionist never would have received him half so romantic. He'd just decided the least he owed her was one more for the road when they heard some other female call out, bright and innocent, "Daisy? Are you back there sneaking a smoke, you naughty thing?"

Longarm stopped what he'd been doing. Daisy didn't as she softly moaned, "Oh, Lord, that's Mavis, back early! She must not have spent her lunch hour with Mr. Corrigan after all!"

"Where are you, Daisy?" their unseen tormentress repeated, as the plump gal speared on Longarm's shaft went right on exhaling and inhaling the same, hissing, "Hurry! Hurry! We can't let her catch us doing this!"

He said, "She's surely going to, if we don't stop, honey!"

But Daisy said she couldn't. So even though he didn't want to, he'd just withdrawn from her and had her standing more sedately with her skirts down when they heard the other gal sliding a key in the lock, and while there wasn't time to button his fool fly he at least had his hat off to cover the same politely as a thinner pretty gal popped in on them to stare slack jawed and demand, "Oh! What are you doing in here and how did you ever get in?"

Daisy didn't seem to know what to say. So Longarm quickly told the higher ranking secretary who he was and added, "I fear your Miss Daisy finds my methods a mite high-handed, Miss Mavis. She tagged along to tell me I couldn't go through your files but, as you can see, I just did."

As he waved about the folder from atop the cabinet, the secretary said in a cool suspicious tone, "So I see. Behind locked doors?"

Longarm soothed, "There's only one door, ma'am, and didn't you notice just now it wasn't locked?"

The gal who'd just unlocked it stared down at the key in her hand in some confusion. As Longarm had hoped she might, she decided, ''That explains why it opened so awkwardly. Just the same, it should have been locked and you had no business pawing through my files without my permission and supervision.''

He assured her he'd never do such a thing no more as, meanwhile, Daisy slipped out discreetly, or thought she had. It was only after they had a little more elbow room back there that Longarm noticed the plump receptionist's underdrawers in one corner. He didn't know what he was supposed to do about such damning evidence at this late date. The more wordly looking Mavis favored him with a cool smile and a wicked twinkle in her eyes as she said, ''Well, all's well that ends well, and I can see why some say you're a diamond in the rough. You'd best be on your way before the boss gets back. I'll see Daisy gets back her unmentionables, and just in case you might care, I get off work at six.''

Chapter 3

"I don't understand," said Doris as she stared pensively out the train window at the rolling sagebrush-covered scenery. "When did we pass through that south pass if the stop ahead is west of the Divide in the South Pass Country?"

Longarm had to allow she had a point as he sat across from her, admiring the way the whipcord riding habit he'd bought for her in Cheyenne hugged her hips. He said, "The true South Pass was a nine-days wonder discovered by early mountain men a mite north of here. Some westbound wagon trains used the handy gap in the Wind River range until someone noticed the peaks gave out entire for a good eighty miles south of the Antelope rises. I reckon it was the confusion between the official South Pass and the general flatness all around that inspired the map makers to dub it the Great Divide Basin or Red Desert, once they had it mapped a mite better."

She wrinkled her pert nose and decided, "You can't tell whether we're in a basin or not. It looks just about like the

35

rolling prairie between Denver and Cheyenne, dear.''

He nodded but said, ''Way more sage and a heap less shortgrass, but I'll allow the country bumps no more dramatically, lucky for the crews who had to string the wires and lay the tracks across a Great Divide a whole heap steeper, everywhere else from Canada to Old Mexico.''

She asked why some called it a red desert, considering how gray-green it really was, and he explained red sandstone bedrock and added, ''See what I mean?'' as they passed through a cut the U.P. must have dug back in the sixties to prove his words today. But the wall of bared earth and rock flashing by their window was more a sun-bleached-pumpkin shade than red.

As she went on staring pensively at the mostly gray-green scenery Doris decided, ''It's not any more a desert than the country down around Durango. I've counted at least a dozen distant cows since we left Cheyenne and they've barely touched all that grass out there so far, this summer.''

He chuckled and said, ''That's because it's sage, not grass. I can see you're from a mining family, despite your kid brother's fancy short chaps. This time of the year even on good range the grass has summer-cured to welcome-mat tan. Sage manages to stay a tad greener because it reaches deeper for such water as may be left where not even a John Deere plow could get at it.''

She nodded and told him a green desert was a contradiction in terms. He shook his head and said, ''It's a good thing you don't work for the U.S. Survey, honey. Land is designated as desert, fit for marginal grazing at best, once they notice you can't grow nothing in the way of cash crops on it. That naturally but not always includes country where the rain don't fall enough to matter. But things can get sneakier than that. You ever been through the Great Salt Desert of western Utah?''

She said she hadn't. He said, ''It wasn't my notion. I was sent in the line of duty. My point is that it rains out on them awesome flat and deadly salt flats about as often as it does on Salt Lake City. The reason they got lawns and shade trees in Salt Lake City ain't got as much to do with watering the soil as it has with what you're watering. Nothing will grow in soil as salty as the Great Salt Desert no matter how much you water it, see?"

She nodded and said, "Nothing seems to want to grow on the mine tailings piling up around Durango of late. Are you saying that's a desert out there, green as it looks to me, because there's too much salt in the soil?"

He started to nod. Then he said. "It's likely more complicated than that, honey. For all I know there's something missing from the soil up here, aside from water, I mean. Some say the climate's just too treacherous for anything but sage and a few tough breeds of bunch grass to make it through a growing season. It's tough to get most anything to grow in thin mountain air that blows so hard, both hot and cold, for no sensible reason even a sagebrush should be able to see."

She said, "It seems to be thriving, no matter how the winds may blow, and didn't someone tell me livestock likes to eat the stuff?"

"Nothing much likes to eat it. It ain't that there's no nourishment in them gray-green stems, it's just that they must taste awful, even to a jackrabbit. Our western sagebrush is no kin to the garden sage you cook with. It's closer in kind to that wormwood Frenchmen use to make liquor taste awful and drive 'em loco."

She laughed and said she might have known he'd know all about disgusting French habits. So that reminded him of some positions they hadn't tried yet, and when their combination stopped to take on water and let them off at Thayer Junction an hour later he was sort of looking forward to bedding down with her some more.

First things coming first, however, Longarm checked their saddles and other gear into the Pacific Hotel, pocketing the key, and took the pretty little thing to supper next door while there was still plenty of daylight left. He ordered fresh eggs aboard fried hash for both of them, having tasted what they called roast beef the last time he'd passed through, and as they waited he told her it might be best if she waited up in their nice new room while he checked in with the local law and dickered some about the ponies they'd be needing from here on north. He said, "You can't discuss horseflesh with ladies present, unless you're willing to pay top dollar for crow bait, I mean."

She said she understood about horse trading but couldn't savvy why he had to jaw with other lawmen this close to the U.P line, asking him, "Didn't you say that sheep baron you have to arrest lives fifty or more miles from here, dearest?"

He nodded but said, "I won't have to arrest him if he just takes the writ from me like a gent. Once he's been properly served it's up to him and his lawyer whether they want to appear in federal court or lose his shirt along with all his sheep range by default. The law down here by the railroad tracks couldn't care less about overstocked range up north of the Tanglewaters. It's still considered unpolite to pack a badge and gun through another lawman's jurisdiction without at least a howdy, and to tell the truth I'd sort of like to have someone covering our backs as we ride on out to the high, wide and empty."

She asked what he meant. He hadn't told her about that bullet whipping past his head in the hall of the Cheyenne Federal Building. He saw no need to upset her with spooky stories this close to her bedtime, bless her sweet but not-too-bright little head. As if to prove his point she asked for no apparent reason at all why they called their hotel the Pacific, seeing they seemed so far from an ocean of any sort up here on the Great Divide.

The waitress was back with their orders, now, so Longarm waited until they'd been served before he picked up a fork and said, "Dig in. We're not smack on the Divide, here in Thayer Junction. Such rain as they get here runs down Bitter Creek into the Green River, which runs into the Colorado on its way to the Sea of Cortez or Gulf of California, which is an arm of the Pacific Ocean, at least. Spit running the other way down the Sweetwater to the Platte, Missouri, Mississippi and so forth takes even longer getting to any ocean, but that don't stop 'em from having an Atlantic Street up in Honeycomb, as you will notice once we get there.''

She dimpled in semi-understanding and said, ''I can't see how the poor water knows which way to run, as tedious as the range seems to sprawl all about us. And if we're on the western slope of the Great Divide now, dear, how come I never noticed as we crossed over it in broad day?''

He washed down some hash with bitter but a mite weak coffee before he told her, ''I reckon at least some falling rain finds the exact location as confounding. There's no mystery between here and the Pacific, or say the stop at Rawlins and the Atlantic. Where we're headed ain't been contour mapped worth mention, and they call the washes we'll be crossing the Tanglewaters because they don't seem to drain no place in particular.''

It was her turn to wash some food down thoughtfully as she tried to fathom the way that might work, failed, and said, ''It seems to me running water has to run some silly place, sooner or later. Where might the washes of your Tanglewaters wind up in the end, if not one ocean or another, dear?''

He shrugged and told her, ''Into the ground, eventually, I reckon. Maybe the thin dry air up here carries a heap of it away in time. It's hardly fair to call such boggy range *my* Tanglewaters. I just told you they've never been properly mapped.''

He dug in on the last of the eggs atop the hash as he added, half to himself, ''That's likely how come the wayward L. J. Travis has been grazing sheep between the Honeycomb Buttes and uncertain limits of the Tanglewaters. He figured nobody working for the BLM was likely to tally his herds anywhere close to accurate in such busted-up stock-scattering country.''

He looked about for their waitress as he added, "He figured wrong. It wasn't the first and it won't be the last time a rugged individualist got caught by government pencil pushers who can add and subtract simple figures on paper. Do you trust me about the two kinds of pie they serve for dessert up here, honey?"

She said she'd trusted him about that silly position down at the hotel in Cheyenne, uncomfortable as it had sounded, at first. So he ordered them the berry pie, explaining, "Apples don't grow within miles of here, so while the berries are fresh picked there's just no saying how long the apples in the apple pie have been mummified to museum standards."

When the berry pie arrived, with more coffee and this time stronger, Doris agreed he surely knew his way around the world and that she could hardly wait to go around the world with him some more. So he demolished his own dessert in unseemly haste, paid the tab, and told her he'd meet up with her later, in Room 2-G, Lord willing and the creeks didn't rise.

Knowing the town lockup stayed open all the time, and knowing how tough it was to judge horseflesh in the dark, Longarm headed next for the town livery to pick out the four ponies he'd need to get him and Doris over to Honeycomb Township. He was braced for the usual bullshit but the old breed in charge was the same cuss he'd dealt with the last time he'd needed a pony suddenly in these parts. So they hardly got to fight at all before Longarm had agreed to a price they both insisted was unfair for two geldings of the paint and roan persuasion along with two mares that came in dapple gray and buckskin. The breed allowed that was an army remount service brand the gray mare was sporting but vigorously denied she'd grown gray in her old age after surviving Sherman's march through Georgia. He insisted, "I'll allow Sherman had 'em playing Rally Round the Flag a lot and everyone knows cavalry bands ride grays, but look at her damned teeth if you don't believe we got her off the cav right after the Shoshone packed it in after that last licking they took in seventy-eight!''

Longarm said he'd noticed the arrow scars, agreed her hind quarters should have rotted off or healed pretty good by now, and said he'd be back in the morning with both the pack and riding saddles the four brutes would be taking turns with all the way to Honeycomb. Then he headed for the town lockup, pleased to note that while his own shadow stretched mighty long ahead of him in the pink dust he'd still made the deal on the ponies with at least half an hour's daylight to spare.

He strode up the plank steps of the town lockup and law office with the setting sun aimed directly at his back. So its reflected glory was glaring smack into his eyes from the window glass of the big front door as he put his left hand to the latch, squinting against the glare. Then he saw the setting sun wasn't the only thing aimed at his back and got out his own gun on the way to the plank porch while the son of a bitch dogging him in the tricky light blew yet another pane of window glass to shards!

But this time, as he lay cussing on his side with his knees drawn up, his balls puckered, and his own .44-40 in hand, Longarm could *see* the back-shooting son of a bitch, sort of, so he fired thrice and saw he'd staggered the tough-to-make-out rascal, albeit he just couldn't say where he'd hit the fuzzy figure outlined by the dazzle of a high-altitude sunset. He fired again as the distant figure crabbed out of sight between two storefronts down that way. Then the door behind Longarm opened inward and the big lawman with one lousy round left in the wheel rolled inside so quickly he spilled the fat boy who'd opened up in the first place.

It was just as well. The kid had come tearing over to the shot-up door with a cocked and loaded riot gun, double barrel and ten-gauge. Fortunately he fired both barrels upward instead of downward as he crashed to the floor atop Longarm. So the only real damage was to the tin ceiling, albeit Longarm found those two gaping holes sobering enough to contemplate as he snapped, "Not me! Him! The son of a bitch I just winged out yonder, I hope. I'm on your side, see?"

The fat kid said he'd be the judge of that, apparently unaware how dumb that sounded, coming from an idiot in bib overalls with an empty shotgun in his pudgy hands. Longarm got up first and disarmed the somewhat confused town deputy as he helped him up as well. When Longarm asked who and what else they had to work with right now the fat boy responded, "There's nobody here this evening but me. It's always quiet this far from either roundup. How come you're loading that pistol, mister?"

Longarm growled, "It's just a chore you're stuck with once you've emptied your wheel in vain at some mother-fucker. I'm not a mister, I'm Deputy Custis Long, federal, and this is the second time today someone's tried to back-shoot me. So do you want to reload, yourself, and give me a hand, or do I have to do every damned thing on my own in this damned territory?"

To the credit of Thayer Junction, the one fool kid they had on duty that evening hauled open a desk drawer to get at two Model '74 .45's in a buscadero gun rig and strap them on, saying, "I've heard tell of you, Longarm. So just point the rascal out to me and we'll have him in no time, dead or alive."

Longarm had six in the wheel, now, but saw no point in holstering his weapon as he growled, "Bueno. But let's see if we can't take him alive. For dead men tell no tales and I'm pretty sure the persistent bastard is working for some-one else. Have you ever heard of L. J. Travis, the biggest sheepman in these parts?"

The kid said, "Nope. But I can see why a sheepman might want you dead, Longarm. For don't our kind hold the same warm feelings for him and his disgusting kind?"

Tracking down sheepmen or shadows at sundown was easier said than done. By the time Longarm and the fat boy had found the dotted line of blood drops leading partway but *only* partway through a slot between the windowless walls of two ajoining buildings, they'd been joined by more than a dozen men and boys who called the fat deputy Freddy and seemed to feel any man who'd back-shoot a visitor to their fair city would eat shit or worse. But while they seemed to know their city better than Longarm, Thayer Junction added up to a surprising number of nooks and crannies for its mighty modest population as the light got ever trickier.

Built mostly of pre-cut lumber by the Union Pacific line to shelter the handful of railroad employees it took to water steam locomotives and determine whether they ought to be sent on cross-country or switched on to the spur line to the somewhat larger town of Superior, Thayer Junction had grown some as merchants, whores and such had moved in to service layover passengers and the surrounding stock spreads. But there were still fewer than two hundred family dwellings, and naturally even fewer business establishments, counting the water tower and tool sheds along the U.P. right-of-way. So where could the son of a bitch be hiding out with his strange face and dripping wounds this late in the game?

It was Longarm who decided, as he bellied up to the bar in the one man-sized saloon with Deputy Freddy and some of the older boys in his ad hoc posse, that they could be making a mystery out of a sore thumb. He explained, "I never got a good look at the cuss and there's no saying how serious I pinked him with a hasty round that could have hit most anywhere. He stopped bleeding, or managed to stop his bleeding, by the time he'd hightailed it less than a hundred yards. So we'd best forget our image of a gunshot fugitive staggering about all puke faced. A change into a fresh shirt over some skillful bandages could hide a multitude of sins."

The fat boy, Freddy, protested, "He still has to look like a stranger, don't he?"

Longarm replied with a thin smile, "Most of you boys

look sort of unfamiliar to me. Can any of you say for sure you'd know the difference between an ordinary looking rider with a Colorado crush to his hat and someone you went to school with for certain? Could you swear half the folk out on the streets of your fair city this evening live and work within your city limits, Freddy?''

The fat boy started to say something dumb. But he wasn't as dumb as he looked. So he nodded thoughtfully and said, ''I follow your drift. All this time we've been tearing hither and yon in search of a bleeding gunslick, the bastard could have been spitting and whittling in plain sight or, hell, searching along with us! I have to confess I only know half our volunteers to nod at. But hold on, your notion just won't work, Longarm, grand as it sounds.''

Longarm asked why. So Freddy proved he hadn't been pinned with his mail-order badge just for being big for his age. He counted on his pudgy fingers as he said, ''Numero uno, you said the same cuss pegged a shot at you down in Cheyenne, earlier.''

Longarm shook his head and pointed out, ''I said *somebody* tried to back-shoot me down yonder. I've yet to get a good look at anybody pegging shots at me. So who's to say the one this evening wasn't waiting up here for me, long enough to look sort of familiar?''

Freddy answered, ''Me. For, segundo, you were shot at in the Federal Building in Cheyenne, even though the odds were fifty-fifty you'd pass on through without bothering to drop by that address. If you need more proof you were followed instead of waited on, consider where you got off this afternoon instead of where you could have, just about as easy.''

Longarm frowned thoughtfully and said, ''I did consider getting off at Wamsutter, an hour's train ride short of Thayer Junction. By pony from there to Honeycomb's about the same distance. But beelining would take me through the boggy heart of the Tanglewaters, and since I have to trend a mite west to get around 'em anyway—''

"The rascal who just shot out our door glass had no way to read your mind," Freddy cut in. "You could have detrained at Wamsutter, just as you could have skipped dropping by the Federal Building in Cheyenne. It'd take a whole army to lay in wait for you in all the places a tumbleweed like yourself might or might not pass through. It makes way more sense that you've been followed. Followed by a yellow-livered sneak afraid to throw down on you more open, see?"

Longarm finished his modest tumbler of plain draft as he mulled Freddy's notions over. Then he said, "You could be right. On the other hand, the real villain behind all this bullshit may *have* a whole army. If it's my most logical suspect we know for a fact he has over a hundred men on his payroll, and a man who'd spend a whole summer up a mountain with a herd of sheep would likely find most any other chore a welcome novelty."

Freddy wrinkled his nose and said, "Ain't no sheepmen in Thayer Junction right now, Longarm. We do get some in town with stock to ship, spring and fall, so it ain't as if we don't know the smell, and I ain't smelled a sheep or sheepman for weeks."

Longarm glanced at the wall clock above the bar as he shook his head to reply, "Don't sound off so cowboy just to keep others from taking you for a railroader, Freddy. Allowing wet sheep smell at least as bad as wet dogs, sheepherders who use soap and water now and again could pass for a cowhand or, hell, a whiskey drummer if they put their mind to it and wore the proper costume. Whatever the cuss we've been looking for looks like, he's too well hidden or too well disguised for us. So I, for one, figure it's past my bedtime and so we'd best say nighty-night."

Freddy protested it wasn't ten o'clock yet. Longarm said he liked to turn in early enough to preserve his beauty. He didn't say he'd lost more than one beauty in his time by showing up a whole lot later than he'd told 'em to expect him back.

So he wasn't too surprised, albeit it didn't exactly delight him, when he entered Room 2-G a few minutes later to find the bed lamp trimmed and Doris already in bed with her face to the wall and her spine staring coldly in his direction. But she seemed to be nude under the thin covers and she'd unbound her hair as well, so the situation might still be salvageable if he could sell her the simple truth.

As he hung his hat on a bedpost and unbuckled his gun rig he softly explained, "It was pure business, honey. You must have heard the gunshots, just at sundown?"

She didn't even sniffle at him. He muttered, "I should have hired two rooms with at least a sofa in the extra one," as he reached for a cheroot, knowing few gals could abide a man enjoying any pleasures they had nothing to do with. But as he struck a light the waxy pallor of the little bare hide he could make out made him lose all interest in tobacco. With the hairs on the back of his neck all atingle Longarm lit the lamp instead of the cheroot gripped between his teeth. Then he reached for her bare shoulder to turn her back over his way. She didn't turn over easy. When she did Longarm gagged and protested, "Aw, come on, Lord, there was no call for you to let such a pretty little thing join the roll up yonder so damned ugly!"

The Lord didn't answer. But Longarm told him someone would, for smashing Doris Drake's face to bloody hash and wringing her pretty neck as well.

Chapter 4

Longarm didn't want to wait for first light. He had to, even though it seemed obvious by midnight that the killer had lit out aboard the town druggist's fine thoroughbred. The bold or leastways desperate son of a bitch had helped himself to cash from the till and medical supplies from the storeroom before helping himself to the druggist's horse as well.

The victim of the killer's lesser crimes that evening might not have noticed so soon, had he not also been the local deputy coroner. Had it not been his duty to view the remains of the late Doris Drake he'd have doubtless never noticed the break-in before breakfast time. He agreed with Deputy Freddy that a hired gun who'd been laying in wait in their town for Longarm and the girl would have surely had his own getaway pony on hand. Longarm only agreed to have a good gander by torchlight at the hoof marks of the missing horse. He spotted a few heel marks that didn't match up with the druggist's low-cut Wellingtons. But one high-heeled Justin tracked much like any other, so the distinctive prints of the long and lanky show horse were more interesting to him.

He knew the odds of cutting any sort of trail by starlight in stirrup-deep sage. So he forced himself to spread out and rest his bones while he gave the killer a chance to make more mistakes. It wasn't easy, even though they'd changed the linens of the bed poor Doris had died in. It wasn't her haunt that kept him awake and cussing until cockcrow. It was her killer still wandering about alive that had Longarm so steamed up. For he had more use for a nasty-by-nature wolverine on four legs than the two-legged kind that'd take out spite on women, children, or other pretty critters as couldn't fight back worth mention.

It didn't help to think about that other killer who'd killed the even prettier Roping Sally up Montana way, or how messy he'd wound up in turn, paying for his crime. Rolling a freight train over Roping Sally's killer hadn't brought her back, and nothing anyone could do to the son of a bitch who'd butchered Doris was going to make her battered body look one lick better. But a man could only do his best and so by the time everyone else in Thayer Junction was sitting up in bed and scratching, Longarm was up and out after the poor gal's killer.

Not having her tagging along, now, Longarm had reshuffled his deal at the livery in favor of the roan gelding and buckskin mare, those two looking most like serious mounts to him. He rode out of town on the roan, leading the buckskin, lightly laden with a few supplies lashed to an Arapho-made packsaddle of bucksin-covered willow root. He only had to circle a mite before he picked up the clear sign left by those fancy horseshoes worn by such an expensive horse. It had been sort of stupid of the jasper to light out on such a distinctive mount. Following the service road east, in line with the U.P. tracks and cross-country telegraph poles, hadn't been all that bright, either. Knowing his quarry had been riding by night as well as way ahead of him, Longarm took advantage of the dawn light and the simple fact that railroads twisted from side to side to avoid going up and down. No broad-gauge locomotive could pull freight worth mention up even a nine-degree grade, so thanks to the westbound runoff this far west, Longarm and his two ponies got to cut across many a rise or draw in more of a beeline than the work crews of the Union Pacific had ever followed.

Making occasional contact with the dusty service road from time to time they still managed to shave good hunks of hither to yon and maybe some time on the son of a bitch before, cutting back down to the roadway just beyond a railroad cut, he failed to spy one fresh hoofprint of any kind. He swore and swung the roan to backtrack until, sure enough, the ever higher sun showed him clearly where the thoroughbred had tried to sort of tiptoe north through the sage and, though the morning dew had about burnt off by now, a big horse moving through sage in the dark did bust the gray-green sprigs pretty good.

Longarm didn't try to follow the spoor inch by inch, any more than a good Indian tracker would have. It was one thing for a redbone hound to follow man or beast with its fool nose to the ground. A human being aboard a pony had to use his brain more than his damned nose, or even his eyes. You trailed a man or any other critter by worrying more where it might be going rather than where it might have been. Even if one could sniff every fool bush along the way, that would still be no way to catch up with anything this side of a snail. So once he had a line on the way the rascal had lit out from the railroad, and made certain it stayed due north a mile or more, he dismounted to tell his ponies as he swapped their saddles, "Our wandering vagabond took a bearing on the North Star. Not a bad move in poor light and uncertain country. Say he left town around midnight and the railroad between two and three in the morning. What are we talking about, say a dozen miles beeline before he lost sight of the stars and had the sun to steer by?"

Neither pony replied. Longarm hadn't expected any advice from them. Once he was aboard the buckskin he just rode on north, spotting a busted sage sprout now and again until, about as far from the tracks as he'd figured, they came upon a bare patch where the thoroughbred had nibbled more sage than Longarm would have expected it to and the cuss who'd stolen it had paused to build a bitty fire of dry grass and pulled-up sage roots. It was easy to see where he'd hunkered by the fire, likely after dawn when he'd have felt safer shedding so much light on the subject. Longarm couldn't tell whether he'd cooked up any breakfast or not. There was a scrap of partly burnt and bloodstained cotton, from a kerchief or shirt, explaining one good reason the cuss might have stopped. Longarm dismounted to unsaddle both brutes and give them a chance to dry their hides and wet their innards with some of the water he'd packed along. He gave each a fistful of oats after they'd been watered, of course, and noticed as he drank down some canned beans and tomato preserves that neither cow pony seemed tempted to nibble at the surrounding sage, even though it was taller and a mite greener in this particular draw. He scuffed out a shallow grave for his breakfast cans as he informed his ponies, "They have to get over to the Tanglewaters, pronto, if we assume the son of a bitch knows where he is. If he doesn't, the carrion crows will catch him soon as we can. The asshole lit out on a mount meant more for fancy stepping than endurance. No sissy thoroughbred would be gnawing sage like a big jackrabbit if its fool rider had thought to pack along grub and water!"

Feeling a heap better about his own chances now, Longarm put his old army McClellan aboard the roan, saying, "The more often I change the longer we'll all last, Red. There's no way cow ponies can outrun a thoroughbred, no offense, but the poor show horse can't last more than a day out here, at any speed, unless the asshole riding it gets to plenty of water and at least some halfway decent grazing."

He mounted up, gave the lead line a firm but gentle tug

to convince the buskskin he and not she knew the way, and headed more to the north-northeast, now. He lit a cheroot and made sure the match was dead for certain as he told his only companions at the moment, "The Tanglewaters are a mite out of our way, as far as serving government writs on range hogs is concerned. But I'm sure even Billy Vail would want us to bring that lady-killing bastard on the thoroughbred to justice, and there's just no way he's ever going to make her all the way to Honeycomb on such a dry and hungry horse. You'll see what a horse heaven the Tanglewaters are, once we get to 'em, even if such boggy range makes for piss-poor traveling!"

He considered breaking out the survey map he'd grubbed off the boys back in Thayer Junction. He considered it a likely waste of time when it came to finding one's way to, from or through the Tanglewaters. Only the main washes had ever been surveyed, and knowing the way runoff drained flat rangelands, Longarm suspected few surveyed washes still ran exactly where they'd first been noticed. One good gully washer could move a streambed a mile to one side or the other. That was how come they called 'em gully washers, and when it did rain up here it rained as if to make up for all the dry times in between.

In theory and maybe in fact, the undecided drainage forming a maze of deep washes and shallow swamps in the northwest quarter of the high, wide and open basin lay about where the spine of the Rocky Mountains would show if it wasn't running deep underground through that stretch. Longarm was just leaving the drainage leading southwest via Bitter Creek and all its branches. If the son of a bitch on that thoroughbred made her through the Tanglewaters, they'd be among the headwaters of the Atlantic-bound Sweetwater. But the killer wasn't likely to get that far, whether Longarm caught up with him before he got bogged or not. Neither Longarm nor any other rider he'd ever talked to about the Tanglewaters knew any way to ride clean through 'em. Looking on the bright side, Longarm knew

51

he didn't have to. He only had to trail the son of a bitch on that sissy horse until neither of 'em could go any farther. Then he only had to ride out the way he'd gone in, with his man facedown over the saddle or, better yet, taken alive to turn states evidence against the son of a bitch he was working for. Longarm knew they'd never in this world hang L. J. Travis just for being a range hog. There had to be some way to prove he'd hired someone to lay for lawmen only trying to do their job.

Anticipating the conversation he meant to hold any day now with the mutton mogul, Longarm smiled wolfishly and declared, "It's no use telling us someone went after me and poor Doris for personal reasons, you dumb bastard. Leave us not forget I'd have never been saddled with this chore if someone hadn't vanished a process server from the land office to begin with!"

Longarm decided it was sort of dumb to argue with a cuss he couldn't even picture. But though he knew better he still pictured the sheep baron dumb faced as any of his sheep, albeit not half as nice. For while it seemed impossible anyone could think it was possible to get away with such high-handed shit, the prisons of this not-too-brilliant world were stuffed with cusses who'd thought they could get away with high-handed shit.

By noon Longarm had lost the trail, or at least he'd ridden a spell without spying hoof-marks or even a sage sprout busted for certain by that stolen thoroughbred. He spied plenty of busted-up sage sprouts and even a bush here and there chewed up just awful. But he spied many a rabbit turd as well, and more than once a pronghorn flashed its white rump at them from a distant rise. So all he really had to go on was common sense, and the assumption the bastard he was after had some. There'd have been critters more worth rounding up for market now and again if there'd have been any running or standing water within miles. The sage was more spread out and only grew shin deep, even down in the draws. So that meant the ground water in these parts was too deep for hand-dug wells, and that explained why there seemed to be no stock or stock spread in sight, even from the higher rises when he reined in for a bird's-eye look-see all about.

Once he spied a white flash way off to their northwest and even shifted his weight in the saddle before he muttered, "Most likely a pronghorn letting us know we've been spotted. Nobody we could be after would be waving white flags at us, and even if he was that loco en la cabeza that's the wrong damned direction!"

He spurred his mount on toward the northeast, trying to convince himself he was still making sense. He knew what he was doing hinged upon the man he was after using common sense, and he didn't even like the son of a bitch.

He paused in a draw to water and grub himself and his ponies as he fought the first twinges of feeling lost. Longarm liked to think he never got lost, albeit, like Dan'l Boone had once admitted, the rest of creation could elude a man a day or so before he figured out where it might have strayed.

As an experienced plains rider, despite his West-by-God Virginia boyhood, Longarm now found it just about impossible to get turned around total in open country like this. He was more worried about chasing nothing much to almost anywhere than he was about spending the coming night as a babe in the woods. Sooner or later Billy Vail expected him to serve the damned writ in his saddlebag on that damned mutton mogul in or about Honeycomb Township, and he knew he was tracking this side issue, if it was a side issue, more by educated guesswork than by any damned sign he'd been able to read for hours.

A crap in the sage, followed by the taste of canned tomatoes and fresh tobacco got him back in shape to press on, riding the roan this time, and after they'd topped eight or ten more rises he noticed the sage ahead grew a mite greener and way higher, even with his saddle swells in places. He patted the roan's neck and told it, "No way we'll see open water this side of sunset, but we're headed right and we just may manage you some sedge grass and arrowhead nuts to nibble if only you'll keep going, Red."

Whether the ponies understood or not, they kept going until the sky to the east was turning more lavender than blue. As the sunset at his back commenced to gild the sage tips all about with the golden glow of Rocky Mountain gloaming, he began to consider a good place to make camp. This close to the center of the big basin, high in the sky as all of it was, a man had to study on where he wanted to spread a bed roll, lest he wake up on the bottom of a sudden lake, should the Thunderbird come flapping before morning. He knew he'd be safe from flooding on top of any of the rises all about. But he was tired of eating cold from the can and liked to smoke before turning in, besides. A night fire or even a match flare could be seen for many a mile in this thin air after dark, and the bastard he was trailing, if he hadn't lost the trail, was a killer who favored creeping up on his victims.

Longarm decided to just ride on as long as the light stayed bright enough to separate the sky ahead from the sage. The first evening star winked on above the horizon ahead. Then, a mite to the north at ground level, he was suddenly aware that a bump on the horizon had to be another rider and, even as Longarm had that figured, the distant cuss reined in atop a rise, as if he'd just noticed something odd as well. So Longarm casually hauled his Winchester from its saddle boot and levered a round into its chamber before bracing it across his lap to ride on in. As he did so he saw the other rider had a Remington Repeater in about the same polite position. It hardly seemed likely a prick who aimed at men's backs and unarmed women's pretty faces would be standing his ground like that, and the pony he was sitting at the moment was a black-and-white paint. As Longarm got close enough to howdy, the stranger howdied back in as cautiously friendly a tone. As Longarm got close enough to make him out better in the tricky light the cuss on the paint appeared to be a breed or maybe a full-blood, albeit dressed just like any other north range cowhand who favored tomato-red shirts and hatbands of Blackfoot beadwork. The breed or assimilated Indian waited until they were within easy conversational range before he said, helpfully, "He's headed for the sometimes-dry passage between Bear Swamp and the Lost Lakes. What did he do?"

Longarm smiled thinly and replied, "If we are discussing a rider on a somewhat taller horse the charge is murder in the hanging degree, for openers. How did you figure me for the law, friend?"

The duskier cowhand replied, "Call me Jim, Jim Two Lodges. You have to be the law because somebody had to be chasing that nervous Nelly on the jaded thoroughbred and who else is out here with us? I'm hunting for a big bay mustang stud who ran off with four mares from our remuda, by the by. I don't reckon you'd have failed to see such a sight, if it passed by you?"

Longarm shook his head and replied, "I haven't seen a horse apple, let alone a strange horse, for many a mile. Does that mean I don't get to hear about the cuss I'm after, Jim?"

Two Lodges chuckled and said, "You're after him a mite to the left of his true trail, albeit your heart is pure and you guessed right about him making for the Tanglewaters. He cut across my bows too far and fast for me to describe him as more than a white man dressed cow aboard a thoroughbred and fancy-dude flat saddle. I waved him a howdy and he replied with a fortunately wild pistol shot. That's how I knew he was on the dodge. Him and that thoroughbred were out of range before I could haul this saddle gun out to reply in kind, more accurate."

Two Lodges twisted to get a better line on the setting sun before he added, "He's got a better than four-hour lead on you if I'm at all right about the time we met up this afternoon. I wouldn't chase him into the Tanglewaters after dark if I were you."

Longarm smiled thinly and shifted the Winchester he was gripping to a more comfortable position as he replied, "He's only got a pistol and I doubt anyone sees better in the dark than me, with the exception of a freak-eyed Mexican I've been told to call El Gato."

Two Lodges insisted, "Pistol shots in the dark from that one out ahead of you might be the least of your worries, lawman. There's some mighty boggy range between here and the higher and drier beyond, and—"

"My ponies have acted surefooted up to now and the starsshine mighty bright up here," Longarm cut in.

Two Lodges shrugged and said, "That may well be. I'd be more worried about Red Sashers or sheep herders after dark on such treacherous range, though."

Longarm laughed incredulously and asked why in thunder a full-grown and well-armed man had to worry about mythical outlaw gangs and hither to harmless sheepherders. The Indian cowboy growled, "There's nothing mythic about the Red Sash Gang and whoever told you sheepherders were harmless hadn't met as many as I have in my time!"

Longarm must not have looked too convinced. Two Lodges scowled and insisted, "Hear me! All the cow spreads have lost many cows this summer and if the Red Sash Gang hasn't been raiding the herds, who else might you have in mind?"

Then he waved his Remington like a schoolmarm's pointer at the empty horizon brooding off to their northeast, adding, "You don't want to ride into any sheep camp after dark, looking half so cow. You know there's always a heap of friction between the morose hermits who enjoy the company of mutton and the rest of the human race. This summer more than heated words have been exchanged and I know for a fact that the Travis outfit has at least one herd grazing somewhere this side of the Tanglewaters."

Longarm whistled softly and said, "They told me L. J. Travis had odd business notions and I'm supposed to take them up with him as soon as I nail the prick who just beat

56

a lady to death in Thayer Junction. But might you be able to illuminate me as to how true or false cow thieves sporting red sashes tie in with range hogging and possibly homicidal sheepherders?''

The Indian cowboy chuckled and said, ''They don't, directly. But hear me, when cowhands on the prod and hunting cow thieves come upon sheep grazing range Wakan Tonka never meant such stinky fuzzballs to graze—''

''I get the picture,'' Longarm cut in. ''I may as well camp here for the night and ride on into all that cross fire with a clear head in the cold gray dawn!''

Chapter 5

Two Lodges stayed for supper and even contributed some pronghorn jerky to the stew pot, but Longarm was just as pleased to see him go when he rode on after that wild stud and its stolen sweethearts. Longarm waited until the Indian cowboy was well on the way south, toward the railroad line, before he shifted camp to another rise and didn't start a second night fire.

For while the friendly talking Two Lodges hadn't seemed to be nursing any bullet wounds or riding any thoroughbreds, he sure had said some mighty odd things.

Longarm didn't find it hard to buy a wild stud running off domestic mares, it had happened a lot, all over the West, since the first Spanish barbs had run off to become *bienes mosteños*, or goods lacking an owner, in Spanish legal terms. The Indian cowboy's tale got taller once one considered he seemed to be tracking more than one set of hoofprints where Longarm hadn't noticed any sign of any kind for quite a ways.

Assuming Two Lodges had some more personal reason for heading south on his lonesome, there was a chance he'd at least been told tales about those infernal outlaw riders sporting red sashes just in case they failed to attract any notice as they loped along the owlhoot trail.

Longarm felt no call to doubt there were cow thieves in Wyoming Territory. Cow thieves went with raising cows, and they'd been doing that a lot up this way since the buffalo and wilder Indians had been thinned some. But the so-called Red Sash Gang dated back to at least the pirates of the Spanish Main. In practice it was easier to talk about a desperado wearing a red sash to show he meant sudden death to anybody getting in his way than it was to track one down in real life. In Cheyenne they'd tell a lawman to seek the Red Sash Gang up along the Powder River. Along the Powder River they'd be just as sure the sons of bitches were raiding out of Jackson Hole. This was the first he'd heard of 'em this far south. He hoped Two Lodges hadn't made it up from whole cloth. For any man who'd tell such whoppers would be as likely to make up tall tales about proddy riders on purloined thoroughbreds, and Longarm *wanted* that son of a bitch to be out there to his northeast, damn his eyes!

He closed his own eyes a spell, sleeping fully dressed with his guns under the covers with him. Awakened before sunrise by a redwing playing alarm clock somewhere in the surrounding sage, Longarm used almost the last of his come-along water to get himself and the two ponies started. By noon they'd used up the last drops in their water bags, and the only sign of natural water was a streak of summer-killed but still tall-standing bluestem winding more or less the same way Longarm was riding. As his ponies enjoyed some of the nutritious straw for noon dinner Longarm told them, "This could be a south fork of Bear Creek we're grazing, ponies. Creeks on the map are sometimes-things in real life in country dry as this. Somewhere ahead we're supposed to come upon Bear Lake, the Lost Lakes, and other lakes as really ought to look more like broad meadowlands right now. I hope you both understand we can't risk grazing more than a few yards out from the sage line, though. I'd just hate to have to haul you both out of quicksand all by myself.''

The phantom spring stream they'd been following ended in a grassy playa not much bigger than a baseball field, however, and Longarm rode around it, muttering to himself as he realized the spring runoff that had occasioned all that bluestem hadn't been one of the serious streams of the Tanglewaters after all. They topped the low sage-covered swell beyond, where Longarm reined in and stood tall as he could in the stirrups for some serious staring at the hazy horizon out ahead. He knew it wouldn't be so hazy at this altitude if a heap of water wasn't evaporating over yonder in the usually bone-dry sunlight. The fact that the swampy Tanglewaters lay over yonder didn't surprise him. He'd lost the killer's damned trail, not his own damned self. He heeled the buckskin forward again, deciding, ''We're more apt to cut sign where progress is more limited by the few ways one can ride through sage and swamp.''

Two miles farther, from atop another low rise, Longarm saw he'd been doing something right. The more gently rolling range ahead was covered with more bunch grass than sage, with more sheep than he felt up to counting grazing north and south of one of those canvas-covered gypsy wagons sheepherders seemed to want to live in. Neither the mule nor runty brown pony grazing on long tethers near the cart could have passed for that thoroughbred. Longarm still felt it best to ride in with his federal badge pinned to his shirtfront and his Winchester held politely but ready for most any sort of welcome.

He saw he'd ridden in about right when a young, reasonably clean but black-bearded and raggedy cuss stepped into view from behind the wagon to yell, ''That's far enough, cowboy!'' and emphasize his words with a brandished ten gauge.

Longarm reined in, but called back, "Leave us not be calling a senior deputy, federal, any breed of meat producer. I'm more interested in a thoroughbred horse and the son of a bitch who stole it than either cows or sheep right now, no offense."

The shotgun toter squinted harder at the front of Longarm's shirt and decided, "You might have come to the right place if we are discussing a skinny son of a bitch on a tall skinny horse of the chestnut persuasion. I may have killed him just this morning. I can't say for certain that chestnut was a thoroughbred, though. I'm a sheepman, not a horse trader."

Longarm moved in closer and said, "I never said you looked like anything else. How come you killed the cuss on the tall chestnut and, if so, where might either of 'em be right now?"

The bearded youth in the sheep-scented raggedy duds pointed off to the northeast with his ten gauge's muzzle, saying, "He shot my sheepdog before I shot him. He had no call to do that. Poor old Spotty was just guarding our sheep from strangers. He wasn't really set to bite nobody. The bastard should have just ridden around if he was proddy about barking dogs. Spotty was *trained* to bark, and you always find barking dogs between yourself and the sheepherder when you ride near sheep."

Longarm nodded and said, "I was wondering why nobody yapped at us, coming in. Might you know what the cuss wanted from you, seeing how easy anyone can see it would have been to go around?"

The bearded youth shrugged and said, "Likely grub or even a change of mounts, now that I see he was on the run from the law. I feared he was just loco when he shot poor Spotty down like, well, a dog. I shot at him right after, of course. So he rode off that way, toward the Lost Lakes, without ever telling me just what had possessed him to act so mean."

Longarm nodded grimly and said, "I'm pretty sure I

winged him in Thayer Junction, night before last. If you winged him as well, he'll be lucky if he makes her far as— How far did you say the Lost Lakes might be?''

The hitherto helpful cuss shrugged and said, ''They wouldn't be lost enough to call Lost Lakes if they stayed more put between spring runoffs. You could likely stumble over a lost lake by sundown, unless you rode between any number of 'em. Either way, there's no saying the gent you're chasing would be waiting for you there. Like I said, I winged him good and he was loping that way, more to the north, the last I saw of the son of a bitch.''

Longarm turned in the saddle to glance down at the torn and dusty stubble between them and the next sage-covered rise, saying, ''A herd of sheep sure leaves a heap more hoofprints than any one horse, but with any luck I ought to cut the rascal's trail a ways out, and either way I'm much obliged.''

As he started to ride on the informative but sort of wistful looking cuss called out, ''Hold on! I know you're obliged to me and I'd be even more obliged to you if you'd help me out with this already spreading herd!''

Longarm reined in, but after a morose gaze about at the sheep nibbling here and bleating yonder he decided, ''I'd be proud to chase your critters into a neater package, amigo mio, but I fail to see just how you'd keep 'em more bunched than they already are, lacking either a sheepdog or stock pen.''

The youth with the problem replied, ''I know. Losing Spotty may have been less painful but no less awkward than losing at least an arm and a leg, when it comes to holding this damned herd together. I dasn't try to move 'em cross-country, and this grass will only hold 'em in this particular part of the country whilst it lasts. You've no doubt heard what Wyoming Territory does to a sheepherder who runs off and leaves a herd of sheep untended?''

Longarm nodded and replied, ''A year and a day at hard labor. Colorado hits you with a swamping fine as well. But

I'd be proud to carry word of your plight to the first telegraph office I come across, leaving you free to play Bo Beep as best you can 'til help arrives.''

The black-bearded youth heaved a sigh of relief and allowed he'd figured Longarm for a gent despite his outfit. Longarm got out his notebook and stub pencil as he asked just whom he had the honor of bailing out, and who he herded all those blamed sheep for. The dogless son of a bitch said to just call him Shorty and added, ''This herd and yon wagon would be the property of Stover Associates. They got one business office in Honeycomb, and of course you can usually get in touch with Miss Kim herself at her home spread up to the foothills of the Wind River. Just address my distress call to Kim Stover, Wyoming Territory, and Western Union will get it to her.''

Longarm didn't doubt that. He grimaced and muttered, ''I thought you'd be more likely employed by one L. J. Travis, the Stovers being cow folk, last time I looked.''

The sheepman who'd just stuck him with a miserable chore indeed said, ''Cows don't thrive as good as sheep on this particular range, and they say Miss Kim owns a coal mine and a couple of lumber mills, once you study on her.''

Longarm growled, ''I just said I know the lady.'' Then, seeing no way to crawfish out of his own given word, he added, ''Give me forty-eight hours or more to make it into the next trail town, Shorty. I savvy the fix you're in, but my first duty is to track down that rascal we both owe so much to and, what the hell, he may win.''

''Now that really cheers the hell out of me,'' sighed Shorty.

So Longarm smiled thinly and said, ''You'd still best try and hold on at least seventy-two hours before you even consider riding in for help on your own.''

Shorty protested, ''I fail to see how I'll ever hold this herd together with no dog to help me, damn it!''

Longarm replied with a fatalistic shrug, ''That's what I just said. You can't be charged with abandoning a herd if the herd abandons you before help can get here. Do you have any salt blocks in your wagon?''

Shorty nodded and said, ''A couple, why? There's no water for 'em this far from the Tanglewater swamps and—''

''There's a heap more water than salt in them sun-cured grass stems they've been nibbling of late,'' Longarm cut in. ''I'd put out a block overnight, praying for rain or at least a heavy dew and fewer coyotes than you have any right to expect in such sage and jackrabbit surroundings. But, hell's bells, why am I lecturing a sheepherder on herding sheep when I got at least one back-shooting cow-dressed son of a bitch getting farther away from me, even as we speak of less important problems.''

Suiting actions to words Longarm heeled the flanks of his mount, tugged the lead line of the roan packing the provisions at the moment, and rode on into the higher sage beyond the already overgrazed grass.

As he did so he noticed some of the damned sheep were already over this way, attracted more by the smell of distant but open water than they could have been by the cheat grass and lesser weeds around the roots of the much taller sage. Being sheep to begin with and domesticated critters as well, their merino blood lines produced more in the way of wool for them than brains. So while they sensed there had to be green pastures and still waters somewhere in this world or the next, they weren't sure which way they really ought to be drifting. But they were certain to drift considerably long before help could arrive even if Kim Stover got Shorty's distress call within the hour.

Longarm knew he was at least another twenty-four hours from the nearest telegraph office, even if he didn't have to look sideways for the wounded killer who'd killed Doris Drake. He'd brought poor dumb Doris along in the fervent hope he wouldn't be even tempted to get in touch with the smarter but way more complicated Kim Stover and now, damn it, he'd gone and given his fool word he'd look her up some more for that sheepherder in distress!

He knew as surely as he knew someday they'd both be dead that if Kim Stover found out he was in Wyoming Territory, sleeping lonesome, she'd make sure she wound up sleeping with him some more, cuss her beautiful blonde hide.

As a general rule Longarm much preferred sleeping with even an ugly lady to sleeping alone, as long as it was understood by all involved that nobody was supposed to wind up moaning in agony about the results. Like most healthy young gents with no more call to make promises than a tumbleweed might feel, Longarm nevertheless had a conscience and knew it was best to pass on gals one was likely to hurt than it was to hurt them, no matter how good it might feel.

The rich Wyoming widow woman who owned all those infernal sheep back there was a sort of north-range answer to the rich and handsome Jessica Starbuck he knew down Texas way, in the same biblical sense, except for the fact Longarm had met Kim Stover somewhat sooner and that unlike the tougher and more wordly Jessie, Kim couldn't seem to face the fact of the cold gray dawns that had to be faced after a really rosy interlude in dreamland with a lover that just wouldn't work as anything more permanent.

Parting tended to be sweet sorrow, even for a knock-around cuss like Longarm, when the pal one had to part from was worth making such good friends with in the first place. But at least Jessie Starbuck and even the stinking rich Monica van Tassel he'd tangled with that time back East could savvy, after only a ladylike amount of weeping and wailing, that no self-respecting federal employee drawing less than a thousand a year had any business proposing to a gal who owned half of Texas or Long Island.

Kim Stover might not own half of Wyoming Territory, yet, but it was only a question of time at the rate she was going. Being widowed, more than once, by halfway prosperous businessmen had given old Kim the grubstake she'd needed to prove the same beautiful figure could hold a passionate body and a head for figures an Arabian rug merchant might have bragged about. He'd already heard about her branching out from beef to mining and construction. The fact she was willing as the cattle barons of both Old and New Mexico to run wool as well as beef on marginal range showed she didn't allow emotions or even public opinion to sway her judgment. So why in thunder couldn't she face the simple fact that they were just grand together in bed but a social disaster anywhere else?

"I never promised Shorty I'd *sign* the damned wire," Longarm told his mount, wondering why he still felt so awful about even thinking of old Kim. It was true he'd lost the protection of poor little Doris Drake's split skirts, God damn the eyes of the bastard who'd beaten her to death, but any town that had a telegraph office was sure to have at least one reasonably pretty female residing closer, way closer, than old Kim's home spread up amid the quivering aspens of the Wind Rivers, so what the hell.

"Who are we bullshitting?" he asked the surrounding sage with a sheepish sigh. "You know damned well that if Kim Stover came a-knocking in her shimmy shirt with all that yellow hair down you'd likely crawl out of bed to let her in with Miss Helen of Troy begging you not to!"

He spied a horse apple and almost rode on, musing, "Of course, if I had old Jessie Starbuck or even Monica van Tassel here to protect me . . ." Then he blinked and reined in to dismount and hunker by the fly-covered object of his sudden inspiration. He gingerly stabbed the turd's dry crust with a finger, noting it was still might fresh for the kind of sun and wind it had been exposed to at least a day. He rose and led his ponies on foot through the waist-high sage and, once he'd cut enough sign to see the horse apple had indeed fallen from that stolen thoroughbred, moving slow and favoring its near forehoof now, Longarm broke out his Winchester, levered a round into its chamber, and let its muzzle take the lead, sharp eyed for sudden movement in such swell cover. For the sage was getting ever higher as the line of steel-shod hoofprints he was following got ever cleaner cut yet harder to follow. The paradox was occasioned by more creeping greenery across the ground even as it grew damp enough to hold hoof marks clear as modeling clay where the hoof had come down on bare soil. The sage began to give way to klamath weed, cockleburs and such as the now flatter range grew ever moister. A springy carpet of chickweed and plantain, or White Man's Footprints as most Indians called it, just about blotted out the trail entire, save damper patches of crushed greenery here and there. Then the trail got easier than ever to follow, albeit not so much fun to follow afoot, as first sedge grass and then no-bullshit tule reeds sprang up from the downright soggy soil ahead.

Longarm remounted before his socks could get really wet and, the Winchester's butt plate braced on one thigh, rode on into what had to be the southwest limits of the Tanglewaters.

The big soggy mess, about forty or fifty miles across and hence a worthy rival of Virginia's Great Dismal Swamp, or a big patch of dangerous tinder fixing to explode, depending on recent rainfall, was tough enough to figure out on a survey map. Staring out across waving tule tops to a hazy horizon maybe six miles off didn't edify one worth mention. By standing tall as he could in the stirrups, Longarm figured he ought to be able to see any other rider within a two-hour walk or half-hour gallop. He didn't see anything out ahead but the swathe of crushed reeds he was following. Following that beat following nothing, of course, and so that was what he was still doing near sundown, having changed ponies some more, when he suddenly spied motion ahead in the tricky light and got the hairs on the back of his neck to simmer down a mite as he made out just what was out yonder about a quarter mile.

The big bay thoroughbred was grazing or drinking, head down and just its back from, say, the hem of its saddle blanket up exposed above the reed tips. What looked at first to be a sort of buffalo hump atop a whatever had evolved to another human figure, rump up and head way down as it went on sleeping, puking, or whatever over yonder.

Longarm circled in from the other rider's rear, Winchester trained and eyes alert to anything that might happen next. But all that happened was the lame thoroughbred catching the scent of company and raising its own head to nicker a happy howdy as its rider never moved a muscle.

Covering the same as he rode in closer, Longarm soon had it figured. The tall drink of water on the stolen show horse was lashed in the saddle, or at least his butt was, with a buckskin riding quirt hooked through both his own belt and its carrying strap attached to the hornless swells of the flat saddle. Longarm could see the cuss had blood as well as crud between the seat of his jeans and the fancy saddle. He still called out, "One false fart and I'll blow another hole in your ass, you asshole!"

But even before he'd reached out to grab the six-gun from the other rider's hip he could see he was disarming a dead man. The cuss was not only wax faced but mighty stiff jointed when Longarm cut the quirt loose to relieve the injured thoroughbred of its needless load. Despite its game hoof and the gratitude it should have felt, the dumb brute splashed on across the sluggish streamlet it had been sipping from when its dead rider landed half in and half out of the water with a muddy splash of its own.

Knowing it wouldn't run far with nightfall coming on and two new pals to play with, Longarm let his own ponies drink as he dismounted to pat the stiff remains down for whatever it had to tell him.

There was dried blood all down the front of the body from rib cage to crotch, but no bullet holes in the black cotton shirt or leather vest. The shirt was a mite tight for him, as cotton shirts got like that unless you bought 'em big enough to begin with. So there was no mistake possible. That tight shirt had been put on *after* he'd been shot.

Longarm unbuttoned the shirt to find out just where that

might have been. He whistled when he spied the bitty blue hole just to the right of the dead man's right nipple. He said, "You sure were one tough son of a bitch for a woman beater. I know I hit you back in Thayer Junction, and there'd be two holes in you and one in your duds if Shorty had aimed as swell as he bragged. So we're talking about you changing your shirt a time or more since last we met, and how come you didn't bandage yourself better, you dumb bastard?"

The dead man wouldn't answer and didn't even seem to want to pack a single scrap of I.D. in his pockets, cuss his mysterious hide. Longarm pocketed the two ten-dollar gold pieces and fifty-odd cents in baser metals the son of a bitch had loose in his own pockets, but the prick had been packing a .32 Harrington & Richardson with ammunition as useless to Longarm, who muttered to the middle-aged cadaver, "Well, I'll keep your ugly features in mind, in the unlikely event we ever find out anything else about you. I had to pay for a decent funeral for Miss Doris Drake, thanks to you, you pile of murderous shit, so you'll just have to forgive my manners if I leave you here to just rot after the carrion crows have enjoyed your yummy parts."

He still felt obliged to kick the cadaver's head into the muddy water as he rose, muttering, "That didn't help, did it, Miss Doris?"

Then, since the thoroughbred hadn't run off any farther than Longarm had expected it to, he remounted, announcing, "All right, ponies, enough of this bullshit and let's get it on up to Honeycomb Township so I can serve that range hog for the BLM, and while I'm at it ask him what he might or might not know about this other cocksucker who took so long to die after I'd shot him!"

He'd ridden due north quite a ways, not wanting to make camp in wet mud no matter how dark it might get, before he suddenly swore and told anyone who'd listen, "Hold on, that just won't work! That one back yonder couldn't have felt strong enough to beat Doris to death after failing to get me! There must have been at least *two* of the sons of bitches, and I've wasted all this time tracking down just *one*!''

Chapter 6

He'd found his way back to sage-covered range in the dark, made all three critters comfortable, and built himself a big enough fire to heat some grub without attracting too many pests before the night winds picked up enough to make him wonder why they hummed like that just off to his right a ways. Suspecting he knew, he took something from a saddlebag that Western Union wished he wouldn't wander about with, and wandered afoot through the sage until the humming of copper wire in the wind led him, sure enough, to a telegraph pole of lodgepole pine.

Shinnying up it in the dark would have been rougher on his Denver tweeds than the denim he'd been smart enough to change into. He still got a splinter or more through his pants before he had an elbow hooked over the cross arm and the old Signal Corps tap-in from his saddlebag connected to the stretch of main line he'd scraped neatly bare with his pocketknife.

There followed the usual bullshit as Longarm cut into the

evening telegraph traffic of Western Union with some government priority business of his own. Some uppity company clerk to the north or south tapped out, imperiously: GET OFF OUR LINE STOP YOU ARE BEGGING FOR PROSECUTION TO THE FULL EXTENT OF THE LAW STOP EXCLAMATION MARK.

To which Longarm replied in his own slow but steady morse code: NO I AINT I AM THE LAW AND MAKE THAT FEDERAL STOP YOUR LINE RIGHT HERE IS ON FEDERAL RANGE AND WOULD YOU LIKE TO STAY IN BUSINESS TONIGHT OR NOT STOP QUESTION MARK.

The telegraph trade had never been noted for sissies since old Sam Morse pirated the notion from old Charley Jackson, who'd rustled it off a French science teacher in turn. So Longarm's warning was dismissed as a threat and replied to with mighty rude remarks about his mother before an older and wiser hand down the line suspected he'd heard that familiar fist on the wire before and tapped out: IF THAT IS PESKY LAWMAN LONGARM HORNING IN IT MAY BE BEST TO HUMOR HIM SO WE CAN GET BACK TO REGULAR TRAFFIC STOP THERE BEING NO FASTER WAY TO GET SUCH A STUBBORN SPARKER OFF OUR LINE COMMA ALAS STOP.

That seemed to help some, even if the relay station at Laramie did interject some downright unpatriotic comments about federal freeloaders. Once they told him to get it over with Longarm sent word to Thayer Junction about the druggist's horse he'd recovered alive if not well, a longer report on the demise of the horse thief to Billy Vail in Denver, along with a request for I.D. if anyone had any wants matching the description, and then, last because he had to but didn't want to, he wired Kim Stover about the fix Shorty and her sheep were in. He addressed it to her business office in Honeycomb instead of her home spread father north and west and saw no need to sign the message, since it was Shorty, not him, who most desired some comforting from old Kim at the moment.

Then, having done his duty he disconnected from the Western Union wire and slid down the pole, slow, lest he impale his morning erection on a pine sliver.

Watering the base of the pole, once he got all the way down it, only helped halfway. Shaking the dew from his lily and buttoning his jeans over the bulge, he muttered, "Serves us right for thinking about Kim Stover after rising from a lonesome bedroll. Old Shorty would likely jerk himself off like a lunatic every payday if he had any notion at all what his boss lady looked like with her skirts up and her hair down!"

As he walked stiffly back to where he'd left his gear and the three ponies in the exceedingly gray dawn indeed, Longarm could see, clear as ever, how much better it was for the wealthy young widow and budding power in local politics to sleep with her own class, if she had to sleep with anybody. Women of any kind were so valued out here in Wyoming Territory they were talking about giving them the vote, come statehood and enough gals to matter in such an empty place. Kim already had more pull with the territorial powers than her mere wealth and beauty might have managed for her in more sissy parts of the country, where men had to deny white women and men of any other color many rights, lest they look as tough. When Kim wasn't weeping and wailing about crude federal deputies just using her poor weak-natured body as a play-pretty, she liked to dream about being the first female governor in these United States and, at the rate she was going he wasn't so sure it was only a dream. He knew that if she was half as good at politics as she was at other skills, Wyoming was in for some mighty sweet administration, if they ever elected such a pretty little thing.

Back by his rumpled bedroll, Longarm inspected the ponies before considering anything else. The two cow ponies he'd started out with were naturally in about the same shape they'd started out in. The thoroughbred, having been relieved of its load and led gently albeit firmly, with its saddle and sweaty saddle cloth toted by the packhorse for now, was perking up a mite, even though Longarm didn't like the looks of that near front hoof.

The tall skinny son of a bitch who'd mistreated poor Doris back in Thayer Junction had neglected to inspect his mount's shoes during trail breaks, assuming he'd even allowed the poor brute all that many, so what had likely started out as a missing nail and a little play in that one shoe had festered to a swollen frog with an ominous oozing from under the steel rim of the shoe.

Longarm got out his knife and braced the hurt critter's pastern between his knees, fetlock and frog up, as he muttered, "Steady, now and let's see if we can relieve some of this pressure. You don't want to walk on this bum hoof, either way, do you?"

Thoroughbreds were not too bright and this one was hurting. So even though the tone of Longarm's voice soothed it some, it still tried to get away or at least bite him as he worked the screwdriving blade between steel and hoof. It took strong wrists. But Longarm had some, and as he pried the steel loose enough to let the puss spurt clear back to the brute's rear hooves, it must have felt about as good as coming to a horse that had been gelded early in the first place. It let out a happy whinny and Longarm said, "You're welcome. That's all we'd best do for you, for now. Come better light and more water to work with I'll see if we can clean things up a mite better. Meanwhile eat your oats and shut up."

Then he rekindled his fire to coffee himself for the tedious day ahead. While the pot perked on sage-root coals he remade his bedroll and got his other possibles ready to go, knowing he had a good many miles and one mighty hurt horse to worry about between where he was and anywhere he had any business being.

By the time the sun was high enough to show him just how tedious the country all around him really looked Longarm had himself wide awake and in the saddle, aboard the roan, with a lit cheroot between his teeth and nothing out ahead of him more interesting, it appeared, than miles and miles of miles and miles.

Every time he was sure they'd made it on through the Tanglewaters, a mile or so of sage rising from dusty thatch would give way to yet another damned canebrake in the middle of what the map distinctly described as a desert, a red one. He took advantage of the lost lakes they kept finding to irrigate the festered hoof of the thoroughbred with some Maryland rye and swamp water almost the same shade of amber. He knew water that dark with tannin from the vegetation in it and the peat under it was too acid for hoof-rot bugs to live in. But the poor brute's pastern still stayed hot and feverish above the hoof, no matter how they tried to keep that festered hoof favored and fairly clean on the trail.

As a skilled horseman of his era was supposed to, Longarm had a fair grasp on equine anatomy. As a man who tended to feel for all law-abiding critters great and small, he was all too aware how it had to feel to the poor brute, once he considered what it would feel like to walk or run through life on one's finger- and toenails.

For that was what the hooves of all hoofed critters were, once you studied on the way their bones really worked inside their so-called legs. Bears walked heel and toe like human beings and other slow but steady walkers. Cats and dogs ran around on tiptoe, while the even faster edible beasts with hooves got about on what amounted to giant fingers, even if they did look like legs at first glance. Hence the mortification the thoroughbred was suffering was much the same as if a giant had smashed his fingernail with a hammer and had to worry about the resulting pussy, black and blue results, while being forced to rest at least some of his weight on the same from time to time.

A cow pony would have known better than to let that bum hoof touch ground at all. The damn-fool thoroughbred kept torturing itself until Longarm was forced to put its saddle back on and tie the hurt hoof up under the saddle cinch with latigo leather. So now the brute just staggered all about on the end of its lead line as if it thought it was a cutthroat trout he'd hooked and meant to fry, alive, once he reeled it in or even led it anywhere sensible.

Thus it came to pass that when Longarm spied a sunflower windmill spinning pinhead small on the far horizon he reined his mount that way without hesitation, even though it was way off to the east and not at all the way he'd been meaning to go. He knew nobody but a stockman or nester set to stay a spell would have gone to the trouble of sinking a well worth wind pumping. The injured thoroughbred would do better left anyplace with a mailing address than hauled on up to Honeycomb, fighting every mile of the way on three fool legs.

They had to cross an unexpected wash, deeper and wider than it had any call to be unless it drained from much higher ground somewhere distant and indefinite. Then Longarm could see the sod roofs around the base of the windmill's spidery frame tower, and when they came upon a two-strand fence of new-looking Glidden wire he grimaced and told his roan, "Damned nesters, trying to prove their homestead claim as farm folk on land I wouldn't bet on raising sheep on!"

As if to prove his point the stirrup-high sage gave way to a good forty acres of ploughed red dirt apparently meant to grow sky-high dust if ever the wind blew really serious in these parts. For since nothing but a few scattered chick-weed shoots had sprouted this late in the short growing season they got up this way, it hardly seemed anything would this side of the first frost.

He still swung all three sets of hooves wide of the neat exercise in futility, even though it meant a tedious detour. For he knew anyone dumb enough to plow forty acres at least twelve thousand feet above sea level would no doubt be dumb enough to drill in seeds as well and, while he knew there was nothing he and the three ponies could do to said seeds that the climate and crows hadn't already taken care of, he didn't want to upset any fools he meant to ask a favor from.

His wide detour forced Longarm to approach the sod house and its outbuildings from their north or blind side, not even a nester being dumb enough to face doors or windows north up here on the Continental Divide. He knew his approach had nonetheless been spotted when a raggedy little gal of around eight came tearing around one corner of the main soddy yelling something at him. Then a man almost as tall and dressed more like a buckaroo than Longarm hove into view, packing a Henry saddle gun, to call the little gal back with a whip-crack warning that made her stop in her tracks as if he'd had her on an invisible leash.

Longarm figured it was none of his own business how others raised their own kids. But he couldn't help noticing, as the little gal turned away to run out of sight some more, that the backs of both her skinny legs were bruised above her bare feet. He still managed to paste a smile across his own face as he rode closer, calling out, "Howdy, neighbor. I answer to Custis Long and I'm bound for Honeycomb Township with these three trail-weary brutes."

The burly brute packing the Henry smiled back, sort of, but said, "You're lost, then. The Honeycomb Buttes and the township named in their honor lie over the horizon directly to the rear of the way you seem headed."

Longarm nodded but said, "I make Honeycomb Township at least another day's ride. That lame bay brute you likely observed following the rest of us around your intended crop of whatever can't make her half that far. Dumb as it's walking right now, it's a thoroughbred of some value, and I don't doubt its rightful owner would be proud to pay you at least a few bucks for holding it here alive until he can reclaim it. I've already wired him I found it for him. As soon as I make it on to Honeycomb I can wire him just where this is, wherever this is."

The rifleman dressed more cow than plow stared dubiously at the gimpy thoroughbred standing head-down on three hooves in the middle distance as he replied, "This'd be the Smithfield spread, me being the lord and master, Sextus Smithfield, Esquire. If we're talking about money, present or future, you'd best come on in for some coffee and cake, at least." Then he called out, "Buddy? Where are you, boy?" and evoked yet another kid around the corner of the soddy. This one was a boy even younger than the girl Longarm had first seen. As he dismounted, his gracious adult host told the kid, "Lead this fine gent's fine critters around to the water tank and make sure they have enough before you run 'em into the corral, you otherwise useless little shit."

The kid didn't argue. Longarm couldn't see any bruises under his bib overalls, but someone had surely smacked him a good one alongside the head recently. The eye was still swollen and figured to get a mite blacker before it ever got a lick lighter.

Longarm wasn't certain he wanted to leave an injured horse in the care of a cuss so casual about the care of children. On the other hand, neither kid looked downright malnourished, and many a confirmed wife beater seemed constitutionally unable to mistreat his horses or hunting dogs. So since the kid was reaching for the reins and lead ropes in any case, Longarm let him take charge of the brutes with an open mind, although he naturally hung on to his saddle gun as the kid led saddle and all away. For an open mind was one thing and total stupidity another.

As he circled the corner of the soddy with the fancifully named Sextus Smithfield, the kid was crossing the dooryard with the three ponies toward the big snare-drum-shaped water tank at the base of the windmill. A buckboard and John Deere riding plow huddled under the low overhang of an open shed between that and the pole corral to the south. Longarm saw the nesters had a mismatched mule team and a couple of cow ponies keeping company there. Old Sextus pointed at the much closer door of the soddy and said, "We'll talk about boarding that thoroughbred over coffee, cake, and maybe some more spirited refreshings if you ain't a Mormon or worse."

So Longarm followed him inside and heard him cussing at someone he called "Woman, dammit," as Longarm's eyes adjusted to the gloomy interior after all that sun-drenched sage.

As they did so he made out that little gal he'd seen before helping an older faded image of herself rustle the refreshings. Old Sextus introduced a man who looked more like himself as Uncle Ralph, even though the lazy-looking cuss lounging in a captain's chair with one spurred boot hooked over a corner of the plank table couldn't have stood a day over twenty and dressed even more like a rider with Pawnee Bill's Wild West Show. Sextus told Longarm to set and make himself to home before turning to the females young and old to ask what was holding up the parade. As Longarm leaned his Winchester against a sideboard of unfinished white pine on the far side of the table he saw a few books, no more than five, well worn and sort of enshrined between gilt plaster bookends on a shelf above. Two of 'em were naturally Good Books, Old and New Testaments, while Gibbon's *Decline and Fall of the Roman Empire* struck him as heavy going for the sort of folk who dwelt in soddies on the Continental Divide, until he considered how much reading time one likely had up here during the six or eight months of blizzard conditions.

The other two books had their gilt titles rubbed too faint to read without squinting rude and nosy, so Longarm sat down with his back to all of 'em as Sextus had Uncle Ralph about filled in on the possible rewards of boarding banged-up horseflesh. For some reason the notion seemed to strike Uncle Ralph mighty amusing. Longarm had come across budding adults wearing chinked chaps and nickel-plated six-guns before. So he didn't ask Uncle Ralph what he found so funny. Skinny young shits with six-guns often felt obliged to defend their own stupidity without considering how stupid they looked to most anyone with half a brain.

The two gals—mother and daughter, he assumed, as he grew more used to both the way they looked and the quiet way they worked together—had the tin plates of chocolate sponge set before the three men at table by now. When the mother murmured the coffee would be ready in just a jiffy, old Sextus at the head of the table growled an order involving the brown jug under the dry sink. As she scurried to fetch it Longarm resisted the impulse to inquire when, if ever, women and children ever got to sit at table in these parts. He knew some Scotch Calvinists of the old school thought it sinful for kids to sit down at the table until they were at least thirteen, and few Plains Indians let their wives and kids eat with them and other menfolk at all. But as the lady of the house poured a tin cup of white lightning for him, Longarm risked thanking her and adding in a desperately casual tone, "This cake sure smells swell. Did you bake it yourself, Miss Lucrece?"

Her face went frog-belly pale but she never let on as she just nodded to him and called out to her daughter, "Sissy, go see what's keeping Buddy all this time."

But old Sextus, closer to the door, snapped, "The boy's doing what I told him to do, Woman. You know the rules of this here house, damn it."

The pallid nester woman nodded soberly and moved back to her cast-iron stove, beckoning the little girl to join her there as the cruder cuss at the head of the table helped himself to a jolt of red-eye and the younger Uncle Ralph cocked a brow at Longarm to quietly ask, "Who told you her name was Lucrece, stranger? May one assume this ain't your first visit to this homestead?"

That seemed to shake old Sextus, too, judging from the way he put down his cup to slither his gun hand out of Longarm's view. Longarm couldn't risk a look-see at the gals off to one side of him. Before the bitty boy could barge in to complicate things even worse, Longarm smiled pleasantly at Uncle Ralph and said, "I never knew this spread was here before. Like yourselves, I spied a distant windmill out in the middle of nowhere. But before I explain further would both you boys mind reaching for the rafters?"

He saw they did indeed, so he fired under the table first at Uncle Ralph and crabbed sideways from his own chair to blast the so-called Sextus in the lower gut as Uncle Ralph crashed backward to the dirt floor, chair and all. Both females were screaming fit to bust between the blasts of Longarm's .44-40 as, having started, he thought it best to just finish the sons of bitches off. So the soddy was sort of filled with brimstone-scented gunsmoke by the time the one front door burst open, and the young mother hunkered in the corner with her bewildered girl screamed, "No, Buddy! Get away from the door!"

But as the kid just stood there, outlined by sun dazzle as the place aired out a mite, Longarm soothed, "It's over, ma'am. It sure was smart of you to tell them saddle tramps this claim had been filed in the names of Sextus and Lucrece Smithfield. But, no offense, don't you reckon you were really stretching your reliance on the classical education of Wyoming Territory?"

The nester gal laughed weakly and confided, "It was a mighty slim straw, I'll allow, but one has to grasp for something when there's just no other hope."

She moved over to the table and sank down in the one chair still upright as her small son in the doorway blurted, "Hey, how did both these Red Sashers wind up on the floor, Mom?"

The woman didn't answer. She had her head down atop her folded arms, and as her shoulders heaved in silent sobbing Longarm told both bewildered kids their mom was surely one sharp woman, pointing at the bookshelf with the muzzle of the six-gun he was reloading as he explained, "When them stinkards rode in to usurp this claim, your well-read mom told 'em the land office had her and your daddy down as Lucrece and Sextus, the Smithfield part being less important.''

Buddy protested, ''Dad's first name was Horace, before he took sick plowing in the spring rain and died on us, I mean.'' As if not to be outdone, Sissy called out from her corner, ''Mama's name is Virginia, not Lucrece, mister.''

Longarm nodded and replied, ''I just said she was smart, didn't I? There's just no telling what even a villain might recall from the Good Book, but your mom figured, correct, as things turned out, someone with a mite more book learning might wonder how in thunder anyone might have ever named a boy-child Sextus. For Sextus the Etruscan was about as low a polecat as you'll find in Gibbon's book on the Roman Empire if you read the whole thing cover to cover.''

Sissy moved over to put a grubby little hand on her mom's heaving shoulder as she asked who Miss Lucrece might add up to in that same thick book. Longarm didn't think the young widow would want her own kids to know all the dirty details, so he just said, ''Lucrece was a proud and highborn Roman lady. After she told her menfolk about the way Sextus had mistreated her she felt obliged to stab herself to death. She knew her menfolk would take care of old Sextus whether she was there or not.''

Young Buddy ran around the table to his mother now, pleading with her not to kill herself, as Sissy told her she didn't have to, Mr. Sextus being stone-cold dead on the floor already. The young widow raised her red-rimmed eyes to meet Longarm's friendly smile. He nodded down at her and said, ''I don't think the real Lucrece had any kids of her own to worry about, and your daughter's right about this version of the story ending less dramatic. I see no call to declare a war to the death on the Etruscan League. So with your permission I mean to bury both these no-goods way down wind a ways.''

Chapter 7

As a lawman sworn to tidy up such troubles Longarm could hardly say the detour to the Smithfield spread had not been worth the time and trouble, albeit he suspected young Buddy enjoyed the informal double funeral more. Kids were always burying box turtles and such in their backyards. When he and the boy got back he explained to the Widow Smithfield, as he washed up at the pump out front, why he'd planted the two villains inside the fence line at the southeast corner of her property. He said, "The one you dubbed Sextus had I.D. that inspired me to open the front of his shirt."

She looked away but went on pumping water over his clay-stained hands as she murmured she knew about the mermaids blowing seashell trumpets on the hairy brute's chest. He said, "That's about enough water, ma'am. As I was saying, the hairy remains added up to one Bowie Bascom who, despite his more recent record as a cow thief, served aboard a Confederate blockade runner during the war back East. If I'm right about that then the young one he told your kids to call Uncle Ralph would have been Concho Landers, a wayward youth who busted out of Leavenworth with Bascom eighteen months ago, before either had served the time they owed for indiscretions in the Indian Nation. We planted 'em not all that deep, where your boy can show anyone who might want to where to dig 'em up some more.''

She made a wry face and demanded to know why anyone would ever want to do such a dreadful thing, adding, ''Had it been up to me I'd have tossed them in Lost Creek after a thundergusher and let the floodwater do with them what it thought best. I don't want to ever think about either of those animals again. So dry your hands on this and let's hear no more about them, if you don't mind.''

He took the clean flour sacking from her but told her, just as stubborn jawed, ''I agree the recent past ain't hardly worth a lady working to remember, ma'am. But you still have a future ahead of you and your boy told me, just now, about his dad coming down with that spring-plowing chill before he could drill in seed-one of the barley crop he'd been planning. You stand to make a few dollars, a very few dollars, boarding that thoroughbred 'til its prosperous proper owner can arrange to take it off your hands.''

She started to say something dumb about how little it cost to care for one more grass-eating critter as Longarm rolled his sleeves back down. He told her, ''Never do nothing free when nobody's asking you to. As I was saying, the pocket change you'll get for that chore won't carry you and the kids through a winter up here. But since my boss frowns on us deputies putting in for bounty money, and since it was you who tipped me off that things here weren't as they appeared, I'm putting you in for the money posted on Bascom and Landers.''

She started to protest. He shushed her, demanding, ''Would you rather Pinkertons and Wells Fargo break their words as sporting gents, ma'am? I suspect the Cattlemen's Protective Association may have bounty money posted on the pests if they were bragging on red sashes as Buddy tells me they were.''

She shrugged and said they'd both bragged so much on so many misdeeds she hadn't paid much attention to their sashes. Then she invited Longarm to come inside and let her and Sissy feed him right. He glanced wistfully at the sky and said, ''If I don't get going I don't see how I'll ever get there, Miss Virginia. Should anyone ask you whether those old boys rode with the Red Sash Gang, just say you can't say for certain and take any bounty money anyone may be handing out, hear?''

She laughed, wansomely, and allowed she could surely use every penny posted on the otherwise mighty useless rascals. Then she brightened and added, ''Wait a minute, I think the older and meaner one, Bowie, *did* say something about some cow crooks sporting red sashes. I wasn't paying that much attention. At the time I was sort of pleading with him to just, well, get it over with and ride on, if you see what I mean.''

Longarm nodded soberly and said, ''He can't pester no ladies that way no more, Miss Virginia. But anything you could recall about red sashes might help if they have any pals in these parts.''

''I'm trying to remember, even though it hurts to remember him that much. He never said he was a paid-up member of any Red Sash Gang. When the younger one, Concho, badgered him about the time they were wasting here—that's what Concho called what they were doing to me, wasting time—Bowie said they had to wait 'til he figured how to get in touch with the good old boys of the Red Sash Gang, as he called them.''

Longarm grimaced and said, ''A cuss like Bowie Bascom would have, whether he knew any such like-minded rascals in these parts or not. To tell it true I've always taken the Red Sash Gang of the north range with a peck of salt. But as long as we're on the distasteful subject, might you recall either Bascom or Landers mentioning *my* name in vain, ma'am? Some outlaws know me better as Longarm than as Deputy Custis Long, by the way.''

She gaped at him to reply, incredulously, ''Good heavens, you're *that* lawman with the last name, Long? I was praying for any lawman to come along, and when you sat down at the table with them like a real rube I thought . . . Never mind. You were slicker than I had any right to hope for, and suffice it to say I'd have remembered if either of those villains had been talking about you before you showed up. Should they have been?''

He shrugged and told her, ''Somebody mighty villainous had one or more gunslicks waiting for me farther south. I fail to see how even a masterful mastermind could have expected me to drop in on you and your kids, no offense, so I'm likely spooking at coincidental crooks. The one I most want can't hardly have a monopoly on murderous skunks in country wild as it gets up this way.''

He knew she was fixing to ask him more about Wyoming gunslingers with or without red sashes if he didn't get cracking, so tempting as her invite to supper and Lord only knew what sort of dessert she had in mind might have been, he saddled up the buckskin, let Buddy help him packsaddle the roan, and got out of there quick as he could, with the three of them swearing never to forget him and he swearing in return he'd put them in for that bounty money before he did another thing in Honeycomb Township.

He meant it. He was composing the wires in his own head as he rode off through the sage to the northwest, not looking back.

Since he was a federal lawman of some rep there was a good chance Virginia Smithfield would be paid off with no more bother to her than she'd already been put through. If anyone did want to dig up the sons of bitches who'd taken turns raping her, the boy, Buddy, knew which fence post to point out, and kids sort of enjoyed that sort of shit. Longarm was reminded of the time back home when the older boys in the eighth grade had decided to dig up Miss

Sally Sikes, the old maid who'd died unloved a dozen years before. Longarm had sometimes wondered what they'd have found under all that West-by-God Virginia loam if the elders who kept an eye on the burying grounds hadn't gotten wind of the adventure planned for that coming Halloween, resulting in considerable birching for would-be ghouls, considering the little fun they'd ever really had with Miss Sally Sikes.

Sunset naturally caught him and the two ponies he had left to worry about somewhere out on the Red Desert, a drier part, with no water to spare for shaving and such after loading the water bag back aboard the buckskin in the morning, half full. For, as he'd noticed taking it down off the roan the night before, when the Red Desert of Wyoming got dry at all it got dry as a mummy's armpits.

He used most of the water left getting himself and the two ponies through most of the day on a seemingly endless expanse of red grit punctuated hither and yon by stunted sage and more thickly by ash-blond clumps of cheat. He thought they were spooking jackrabbits now and again, but every time something bounded out of the cheat grass as if to prove it was worth eating, after all, the bounding fuzz ball turned out to be tumble mustard on second glance. It was too blamed dry for the more serious looking tumble*weed* out here where the range seemed rain shadowed by the distant purple peaks of the southernmost Wind Rivers. Or maybe the red soil of these parts simply didn't hold enough moisture between rains. It rained a heap up this way, considering how parched it could look, even where water did run by between wet spells.

About the time he was considering another night bedded down on red dust, without much enthusiasm, Longarm topped a rise to spy the grotesque formations of the Honeycomb Buttes, too far off to his north-northwest to make out in detail. But when he considered the township of Honeycomb had to lie somewhere out there between where he was and where the Honeycomb Buttes rose, even farther off, he told his ponies, "We're going to punch on through and to hell with how late after sundown we make it. For I don't know about you, but I've had me just about enough of this infernal range as can't make up its mind to be dust dune or canebrake. So let's just get back to civilization if it takes half the night, hear?"

In point of fact it was closer to ten P.M. than midnight when Longarm finally reined in before the big red barnlike structure with HONEYCOMB LIVERY lettered on it in an attempt at gold that had come out more a shade of mustard. He still tipped the old geezer on night duty an extra nickel a head with orders to make sure both ponies were watered well before they were oated. The old geezer cackled that he preferred to see ponies swollen like expectant cats with oat bloat, so Longarm knew he'd left the brutes in safe hands as he packed his McClellan across to the Beehive Hotel to safely store his Winchester and other valuables before heading for the Western Union office down the street.

That was when he began to wonder whether he and the ponies had really punched on through to civilization. The vapidly pretty but no-longer-young lady behind the hotel desk told him not to be silly when he asked if they had rooms with baths to let. She said he could sleep by himself or with a friend of his own choosing behind a door that really locked, if he was willing to spring for a whole silver dollar and, when he protested that seemed steep for such accommodations she just nodded and replied, "You'd be right, if this was Wamsutter, Lander, or any other big Wyoming metropolis with competition to worry about."

He cocked a brow to ask if it was safe to assume the Beehive was the one and only hotel in Honeycomb, and wasn't too surprised when she replied, "Only hotel for a hard day's ride in any direction, sport."

So he snapped a silver cartwheel on the zinc countertop near the guest book and proceeded to sign the infernal book with the pencil provided by the management. She handed

him a key in return but neither she nor anyone else offered
to show him the way up to his hired room. He got to find
his own way, saddle and all, but, looking on the bright side,
it saved him the dime tip a bellhop would have expected in
such a fancy hotel.

The room, once he found it, was spartan as he expected
but somewhat cleaner, and while there wasn't even a crapper
on the same floor they had provided a chamber pot under
the brass bedstead and an ewer of water atop the washstand
in one corner.

He hung his saddle and possibles over the foot of the
bed. Since he had to go out again and the summer nights
at high altitude were nippy as October at sea level, he broke
out a sheepskin jacket to wear over his shirtsleeves and
cross-draw rig. He let it hang open. It didn't get *that* cold
up here, most summer nights.

Locking up and pocketing the key, Longarm went back
downstairs, where the night clerk called him back to her
desk, and for a moment he feared they were going to have
a dumb discussion about the key in his pocket. Some few
small-town hotel clerks couldn't see it saved needless toil
and discussion when guests simply let themselves in or out
as need be. As he approached the desk he could see by the
one lobby lamp hanging over it that she'd run a comb or at
least some fingers through her pine-bark colored hair and
either pinched or rubbed some fresh rouge on her cheeks.
She smiled at him sort of flutter lashed to say, "I didn't
know who you were until I had a chance to go over your
sign-in just now, Deputy Long from the Denver District
Court!"

He smiled sheepishly and allowed it was his own fault
for forgetting his real name was John Smith, adding that he
didn't know he was all that famous this far from home.

She confided, "To tell the truth, I'd never heard of you
before this morning. The rich young Widow Stover told me
all about you when she stopped by to ask if you'd ridden
into town yet."

Longarm started to ask a dumb question. Then he nodded soberly and answered, partly to himself, "Right. I wired sort of public that I was bound for here and this is the only hotel I could check into." Then he added, with a confidential smile, "I'd just as soon that particular lady never knew I was staying here, if you follow my drift."

The attractive but far less lovely lady behind the night desk dimpled and confided back to him, "I thought it had to be something like that. Miss Kim was trying too hard to look like butter wouldn't melt in her mouth as she inquired sweet and innocent about you. You must really be the bee's knees with the lamps trimmed, despite how rough and ready you come across where a gal can see you sneaking up on her."

Longarm laughed and replied, "My relationship with the rich young Widow Stover ain't all that sneaky. It's just that I'm only passing through on serious government business and, well, I don't have time for social stuff, see?"

She said she savvied but added, "Who am I to call a paid-up guest of this establishment a barefaced liar?" So he said he'd make it up to her before he checked out if she'd keep his little secret for him.

Then he strode on out to the darker street before she could set a particular price on her silence. He knew it was a mite late to kick himself for signing in under his true identity, even if a good swift kick would have helped, this late in the game.

Old Kim was smart as well as warm natured. He knew now he should have known then she'd check with Western Union whether he signed his message about her dogless sheepherder or not. Western Union had a firm policy against divulging private information about its paying customers, they said, but he hadn't paid them for the use of their lines to begin with, and he'd long since established in the second place that some telegraph clerks could be persuaded to bend the rules by a stubborn lawman, or maybe a stubborn gal as owned half the damned territory and no doubt at least some telegraph stock.

The damage being done, if that clerk back at the hotel gave the show away to another female, Longarm could only go on about his business as per departmental regulations. First things coming first he strode down to the Honeycomb marshal's office and lockup to inform the local law he was on their claim with a writ he meant to serve on a local voting man.

He wasn't surprised when he got there to discover Marshal Preston, the boss man, had not only left for the night but couldn't be found at any particular home address unless and until he got lucky, Marshal Preston being a single gent no older than Longarm and apparently just as fond of a good time, off duty. So Longarm told the two night men on duty there who he was and why he was in town. The gray geezer seated in the marshal's chair with his feet up on the desk said they'd be proud to tell their boss, if he ever showed up again, but added that Preston wasn't going to like it and had a sort of uncertain temper.

Longarm smiled thinly and told them both, "I've been known to cloud up and rain all over assholes arguing jurisdiction with me, too. Might I inquire just what sort of an in old L. J. Travis might have with you boys and your testy boss?"

The gray geezer didn't answer. The younger one lounging against a rifle rack in one corner grimaced and growled, "That'll be the day when old Dodge Preston sticks his neck out for a fucking *sheepman*!"

So Longarm allowed he found that even more confusing and the gray one behind the desk explained, "Marshal Preston's a cowman, like you, me, and most white men in these parts. Travis is some sort of breed and half cracked besides. You won't find him at his home spread by the Honeycomb Buttes. He's somewhere out on the open range and on the prod as well they say. So if you track him down out yonder with your damned old writ from the BLM, you're just about certain to be served a kill-or-be-killed situation in return, see?''

Longarm looked about as puzzled as annoyed when he replied, ''I'll be switched with snakes if I see any sense at all to what you just now said! The land office warned me I might have trouble with the range-hogging mutton mogul. You tell me he's not on any better terms with you and yours. So why in thunder should your boss give a fig if I have to straighten the surly sheepman out a mite?''

The gray town deputy replied, ''Your rep has preceded you, Longarm. We know all too well how things have to turn out if L. J. Travis and his sheep-screwing rabble are expecting you, and this does happen to be an election year, if you take my meaning.''

Longarm grimaced and said, ''I'm commencing to. No matter how your boss feels about sheep and sheepmen, personal, there must be one hell of a heap of mutton on the Red Desert range about now.''

The one with his elbow hooked over the corner of the rifle rack chimed in, ''They told us you was an old pro, Longarm. You know getting backing from the courthouse gang can be more vital to a lawman than how quick he can draw and fire. Wyoming Territory lets even sheepmen vote, and you was all too right about how many of the pests we have in this corner of Wyoming.''

The older one sitting down added, ''Our orders are to stay on good terms with both breeds of stockmen. Lord knows it ain't easy. For even some of the cowmen have commenced to act proddy as hell and I just don't see how we'll ever avoid taking one side or the other, once all this resentment about range comes to a head and, well, pops.''

Longarm said he hadn't heard they were planning a range war in these parts, this summer, adding, ''Seems to me it was only a few short years ago that all the whites of any persuasion were standing shoulder to shoulder against the Shoshone and Bannock.''

The older deputy shrugged and said, ''We live in changing times. It ain't the persuasion of the stockmen as causes friction half as much as the persuasion of said stock. The Red Desert's marginal range for cows, even if you keep 'em moving from water to water before they can overgraze such grass as there is out yonder. You know how sheep cut up everything they don't eat entire with them wicked little hooves of their's.''

Longarm knew no such thing, but arguing the question with men who'd been told sheep and cattle were natural rivals was futile as arguing any other religious point. So he told them he still had to send a night letter to his own boss and left for the Western Union office. As he strode the plank walk alongside the dust-paved main street he could see why the local law was on edge about the delicate balance between cowhand and sheepherder in these parts. There was some overlap in working costume, of course. Fights could and did result from a cowhand being mistaken for a sheepherder, and vice versa. How often depended on how hard the feelings might be between the two sides. Longarm knew the dislike between sheep and cow folk was carried to downright loco lengths north of, say, the Arkansas River on one side of the Rockies and, say, the Gunnison on the other. Neither Mexican stockmen nor most Anglos who'd been taught the skills of raising stock on land not good for much else by the original experts on the subject seemed to get half so excited about what a neighbor might or might not want to raise, as long as he didn't mess with other men's womenkind or horseflesh. The Afro-Hispanic longhorn cow, the merino sheep and of course the Arab and Barb breeds of cow pony had all come over to the New World with the Spanish, who, left to their druthers, preferred pork and chicken to eat in any case. Legends were still told of pig drives to rival any up the Goodnight Trail as the early Spanish-speaking rancheros spread out across the semi-arid sort of country they and their stock seemed to thrive so well in. The vaquero had only become the modern buckaroo with such a self-conscious distaste for anything but cows and horses after beef-eating Anglo Saxons had taken up the trade, along with most of the Far West, after the Mexican War.

He knew stock breeders in other parts, and smart ones like Kim Stover, even up this way, ran sheep and cows together on range they knew how to manage. Given their own druthers, cows preferred to eat grass while sheep liked leafy forbs and weeds better. They only competed seriously enough to matter when forced by overstocking to just eat whatever was there, the cows skimming chickweed and the sheep mowing cheat grass close as they were accused of. So Longarm found it easy not to take sides in the gut-and-git operations of range hogs. For while he preferred the perfume of cowshit to that of sheepshit and liked the chores of a cowhand more than those of the farmboy he'd been born in West-by-God Virginia, he knew as a lawman how often pure greed lay at the heart of such proddy bull.

So he was still brooding on man's often pointless inhumanity to his fellow man when, having gotten off a night letter to Billy Vail at the Western Union, he parted the batwings of a nameless saloon between the telegraph office and his hotel for a nightcap and maybe a sandwich, if they served anything but firewater.

They did. So Longarm wound up standing near the potbellied stove near the back of the rinky-dink shoe-box saloon with a beer schooner in one hand and a ham on rye in the other, idly watching a poker game with his back to the bar. That would have been that had not a young squirt wearing a snakeskin hatband on his black Stetson and a brace of Smith & Wesson .45's on his leather-clad hips sniffed loudly to ask in a dramatic tone whether anyone else back there smelled a dead and decaying sheepherder.

Since Longarm hadn't even noticed a dead Indian back near the stove he just went on stuffing his face until the wiseass moved between him and the stove to declare, "I'm talking to *you*, pilgrim. How dast you come in here with that damned wool-lined jacket on? Does this look like a hangout for infernal sheepherders?"

Conversation around the nearby poker table ceased as Longarm asked his accuser, conversationally, "Might you have been in or about the Chapman Saloon in Durango the evening I had about as dumb a conversation with a cuss of similar disposition, sonny?"

The kid blustered, "We never met in Durango or no place else, you sheep-fucking son of a—"

Then he was spinning on one leg like a toe dancer with a hot .44-40 slug in the shoulder of his gun arm. For there were things a grown man might abide and there were things he just couldn't, and Longarm had always had a heap of respect for his mother.

He'd naturally just let go the sandwich in one hand and the beer schooner in the other when he felt the call to teach the little shit some manners. So he had nothing in his own hands but his smoking six-gun when the more confused than hurting target of his wrath instinctively grabbed for the stovepipe with his bare hands to keep from belly flopping atop the red-hot cast iron.

He knew he was hurt, then. As he filled that end of the saloon with girlish wails and the stench of scorching flesh, one of the poker players who hadn't dropped his beer to the sawdust-covered floor rose with his schooner full and poured the contents over the hands of the screaming young gunslick as Longarm hauled him back from the stove by the collar of his shirt and, when he still kept screaming, pistolwhipped him skillfully and not unkindly unconscious.

In the sudden silence that ensued the good-looking young cuss who'd sacrificed a whole pint of beer for decorum smiled wearily at Longarm and announced, "I'd be Dodge Preston, Marshal of this here city, so don't say you weren't warned after you reply to my officious question as to your exact intent just now."

Longarm said, "Nothing all that mysterious transpired, Marshal. You and these other gents must have heard the asshole calling me a sheepherder and winding up to call me worse."

Preston stared soberly down at the youth sprawled at their feet in the sawdust as he insisted, "The question before the house is whether we want to charge you with simple assault or attempted murder. Meanwhile you'd best hand me that side arm so we can all talk more relaxed."

Longarm hauled out his billfold instead, muttering, "There must be some sort of brain fever going around up here in the high country. This boy started up with me for no sensible reason I could see. I let him live, anyway, and now I have another gent growling war talk at me while I'm standing here with the damned drop on him!"

Dodge Preston took the billfold for a closer gander at Longarm's federal badge and I.D. Then he handed it back with a devil-may-care grin, saying, "Seeing we're both the law, we'll just never know whether I could have taken you or not, and I was feeling sort of curious, too."

Chapter 8

Once they got the gun waddy over to the town lockup it developed that while Marshal Preston and his own deputies had seen the pest around town of late, and thought his handle might be Sandy, nobody could say much more about him. So while the doc put bear grease and bandages on his paws in the back, Longarm and the others pawed through Wanted fliers out front. Preston got to do so at his desk, of course, while Longarm got to sit on an ammunition case with a pasteboard box of fliers, recent and not so recent, as he brought the town law up to date on his reasons for being up this way and the curious adventures he'd had getting even this far.

Preston agreed it was up to the Widow Stover to get help to her dogless sheepherder, and that he didn't want the chore of collecting bounty money for the Widow Smithfield as long as Billy Vail and old Henry down at the Denver office were willing to bother with the damned paperwork. He knew where the Smithfield spread was and said he'd give directions gladly enough to anyone that Thayer Junction druggist sent to fetch his purloined thoroughbred. When Longarm asked whether Preston and his boys had heard tell of the Red Sash Gang prowling the Red Desert this summer, Preston snorted and said, "Not last summer, neither. They're supposed to be over in the Powder River country, albeit the first time I heard tell of 'em they were supposed to be raiding in Kansas for either the North or the South, depending on who was mentioning their name in vain. I never saw any white man with a red sash around his middle, back there or out here."

Longarm murmured, "I was wondering how a Wyoming lawman had been named after a town in Kansas. There's nothing about red sashes in connection with all these unruly rascals wanted so bad by so many. But there must be some sort of trouble brewing up this way this summer, pard. I started out with a land office writ the land office seems afraid to serve themselves, and I've sure run across a heap of hardcase strangers when you consider how unpopulated most of this country's supposed to be."

Dodge Preston proved he'd been listening as well as reading when he replied, "The one as tried to back-shoot you down to Thayer Junction and beat your gal to death when that didn't work could have been a pal of her mean brother, Kid Chinks. For that matter, it could have been Kid Chinks in the flesh, since you never got a good look at him and some old boys have been known to get mighty vexed with a sister who's been, ah, getting close with the law."

Longarm grimaced and said, "Already thought of that. The notion of my having winged Kid Chinks in Thayer Junction falls apart as soon as I track down the cuss to find him another cuss entire. In case you forgot, I knew Kid Chinks on sight. I'd never seen the older and much taller cuss sitting dead in the saddle of that stolen thoroughbred."

Preston turned over yet another reward poster to gaze morosely down at the ugly woodcut of yet another mean bastard as he insisted, "You can't be certain there was only

100

one cuss after you in Thayer Junction. Didn't that sheep-herder say he pegged a round or more at the tall rider you finally caught up with?''

Longarm nodded but said, "He never really hit the rascal. He no doubt thought he did. The cuss was already hurt and may have flinched or even cried out when yet another round passed close to his delicate hide. But he'd put a fresh shirt on over the hole I'd put in him much sooner.''

"If it was you and not someone else, you mean," said Preston. "Hey, I think I've seen this here Barbarosa Brown passing through, unless it was some other scar-faced mutt with a red beard. Says on his yellow sheets he's a stock thief, too!''

Longarm soothed, "He was. Past tense. The Rangers caught Barbarosa Brown in the company of some Texas cows bound for Mexico, late last fall. He elected to shoot it out and guess who won.''

Then he fished out a cheroot as he continued, "Getting back to my trailing that limping thoroughbred from about where I first swapped shots with someone to where I found someone, dead, aboard said stolen horse, the two outlaws I had it out with at the Smithfield spread couldn't have been tied in with Kid Chinks or any other mean little Kid who was sore at me, personal. Bowie Bascom and Concho Landers were full-grown habitual criminals with no known connection to Durango or the pool hall gun waddies Kid Chinks hung around with. It gets even more sinister when you consider the Widow Smithfield told me she'd heard them jawing about Wyoming pals sporting red sashes.''

Preston shrugged and said, "Hell, we all bullshit when we got a female listening to us. I wish you'd leave off trying to make a mystery out of a dung hill, Longarm. We got plenty of trouble up here on the Red Desert range without anyone having to creep about in red sashes.''

Longarm said he was all ears and that trouble on federal range was as much his business as anyone else's. So Preston sighed and said, "Shit, you just bumped noses with some of it, Longarm. Too many stockmen have been crowding in on limited grazing, with or without permission from the BLM, and nobody would take the position of Brand Inspector now, even if it paid a living wage."

Longarm nodded and said, "I've heard the handy excuses either side might use to justify running off at least half the competition for limited resources. Leaving aside your own tastes in shit on your boot heels, pard, which side would you fault most for the trouble brewing up in these parts?"

Preston didn't hesitate. He said, flatly, "The sheepmen. The ones in with that infernal L. J. Travis, leastways. I ain't saying that as a reformed cowhand. I'm saying it as a lawman who's received all too many bitches about stolen cows and hardly any on stolen sheep."

Longarm lit his cheroot and got it going good before he soberly replied, "I wouldn't be up this way if Travis paid his range fees like a good little boy. But he got caught as a range hog selling way too many sheep, not cows, of late. So might that not prove him less guilty than, say, a big cattle baron who's been shipping an unusual amount of beef?"

Preston shrugged and said, "If we had enough evidence to nail it on anybody they'd be in the back with that young shit you shot and singed this evening. Stolen stock is more the business of the county sheriff's department, anyway. I just have to keep the peace between cowmen, sheepmen, and any strangers passing through that either side might want to pat down for running irons or that paint that sticks to wool come rain or shine. As you saw just a short while ago in that saloon, it ain't easy."

Longarm didn't answer. The portly old sawbones they'd sent for was coming out from the patent cells in the back. Longarm rose to ask the doc how their customer was doing. The doc shrugged and said, "The flesh wound in his shoulder ought to heal good as new in six or eight weeks. His hands are liable to take longer and he may need some simple but not too comfortable surgery before he ever uses that right hand for any chore requiring skill."

Longarm asked what was busted. The doc explained, "Nothing. But when you sear fingers almost down to the bone they tend to heal, when and if they heal, sort of, well, webbed together a mite and mighty stiff whether stuck together or not."

The older man glanced at the Regulator brand clock on the wall and added, "There's not much more I can do for him, tonight. I left him some opium for the pain and if that don't put him to sleep feel free to feed him some whiskey as well. I just told him to look on the bright side when it gets to really hurting. As long as he can feel pain we'll know gangrene ain't set in yet."

The doc left. Preston started to get out more Wanted fliers, but Longarm said, "Hold on. Why don't we find out what the boy has to say for his fool self and any friends he might have before he gets too feverish to make sense?"

Preston was willing. He led the way back to the cell block but didn't bother to unlock the bars when the kid came over to them, one arm in a sling and both hands bandaged big as if he had on boxing gloves. He glared at them both as he declared in a tone midway between a whimper and a growl, "The doc says you boys have crippled me up just awful and, soon as I can get me a lawyer I aim to sue the shit outta you, hear?"

Preston muttered, "Hang some crepe on your nose, Sandy. Your brain just passed away entire."

Longarm said, in a kinder tone, "I was the one as shot you, nicer than you deserved. It was your own grand notion to grab hold of a hot stovepipe and if the marshal, here, hadn't donated his own beer to treat your self-inflicted injury you'd be hurt a lot worse."

Sandy still insisted he meant to sue the township, county, and Wyoming Territory. Before Preston could cuss back Longarm soothed them both with, "It's a free country and of course you may just live long enough to get yourself a lawyer, once old Dodge here lets you go, with or without your famous guns strapped about your famous ass."

The young gunslick looked confused by Longarm's friendly words. Dodge Preston proved how much wiser to the ways of a wicked world he was by observing, "I got no call to keep his guns, Longarm. You heard the doc say he'll never be able to handle 'em so hot without a heap of time and tender loving treatment."

Longarm nodded and said, "I was hoping you'd see things my way, pard. I got too much serious business on my plate to appear in court against this piss ant, and letting his own kind take care of him will cost the taxpayers less in the long run."

Sandy gulped and said, "Hold on, now. Who said anything about anyone else being after me?"

Preston laughed, sort of mean, and said, "I was right. Your brains are long gone, if you ever had any. Why in thunder did you ever start up with a well-known gunfighter like Longarm, here, if you didn't plan on leaving Honeycomb a famous gunfighter in your own right?"

Sandy gulped, grinned sheepishly, and tried, "I never meant to really hurt nobody serious. They only told me to run this big moose out of the territory. They never told me who he was and, man, I have never in my life seen anybody draw and fire half so sudden. Had I known I was up against anybody half so good I wouldn't have gone up against him for double the money, and I swear I'll never do it again if we can all be pals now."

The two lawmen exchanged glances. Longarm asked the prisoner who he'd meant by the "they" who'd inspired the nonsense in the saloon. Sandy tried, "Just a sporting gent who said his name was Joe. Never said if he had any last name to go with it. He fibbed to me about you and that sheepskin jacket, too. Said you was a range inspector shaking him down for grazing fees he didn't owe. Said he'd make it worth my while if I could maybe persuade you to leave for the low country."

While Longarm pondered that a mite Preston demanded, "Might this mysterious range-hogging Joe be sixty or so

104

with crispy gray hair and maybe a dip of the tar brush to his features?''

The Celtic-jawed Sandy blinked in confusion at the delicate way the older boy who'd grown up in a border state had put that. So Longarm explained, ''Old Dodge, here, meant to ask you if the gent looked as if he might have some colored blood. I was told a certain mutton mogul was sort of dark featured, too, come to study on it.''

Sandy frowned thoughtfully and decided, ''I'd hate to bet money on it, either way. He was older than any of us here, and his hair might have been most any color. I never laid eyes on him in sunlight or even bright lamplight, to tell the truth.''

Longarm took Preston aside to mutter, ''He wouldn't know how to tell the truth if it was in his favor. We'd best let him bake in his cell overnight. Eating opium pills and looking forward to a short spell of fame as a gunslick who can't cock a gun with one hand ought to convince him of the error of his ways.''

Dodge Preston nodded but muttered back, ''Let's hope you're right. I can see why you can't afford to press charges. I hope you can see I can't hold him against a writ of habeas corpus unless you do!''

Longarm started to say something dumb about an arrest on suspicion alone being good for at least seventy-two hours. Then he said, ''We don't want to hold him all that long. Leastways, I don't. What say you bust him loose, feeling even worse, after the two of us have enjoyed some sleep and I can trail the sneaky little shit in broad-ass daylight?''

Preston said, ''Come morning he'll likely be too feverish to leave under his own power, if I recall my own bullet wounds right.''

So Longarm said, ''Bueno. Given some tincture of cocoa leaf to put him on his dizzy feet, he ought to just stagger out to scout up his pals without even looking back.''

Preston replied, dubiously, ''We got some tonic we can

feed him with his beans in the morning. But what if such a quick cure kills him?"

To which Longarm could only reply with a fatalistic shrug, "Shit, he was out to kill me, wasn't he?"

Back at his hotel, Longarm was informed by the sort of drab but mighty friendly female at the desk that he'd just missed something more spectacular. She told him, "That rich Window Stover sure must want to see you, Deputy Long. She as much as called me a liar when I told her you weren't staying with us. I don't mind saying it was tempting when she commenced to tap a ten-dollar gold piece on this very desktop. But like old Boss Cameron said when he was running Penn State for the Republicans, an honest woman is one who stays bought."

Longarm laughed and got out a half-eagle of his own to spin atop the zinc top. As it spun down he told her, "I think his definition was that of an honest *politician*, but your point's well taken and raises some interesting angles indeed."

As she deftly scooped the coin up she replied, "I know. That's why I included sneaks of my own sex. You told me you'd make it up to me if I defended you from that beautiful blonde and I was banking on you being a man of your word."

He told her she'd done right and went on upstairs to see if he could catch those forty winks at last.

He couldn't. He started out sensible enough. Leaving the lamps out just in case anyone was out there in the night with a rifle and a grudge, Longarm stripped and gave himself a whore bath at the corner washstand. Then he made certain the door was locked, his six-gun and Winchester were handy to the head of the bed, and his double-shot derringer was tucked between the mattress and the headboard before he rolled under the covers naked and goosebumped from the chill night air, to count some cows. He didn't even want to think about sheep right now.

106

Counting backward as he backed the stock over the stone wall helped a heap. For soon that old stone wall looked more familiar and the cows leaping backward over it had turned into retreating troopers and it was hard to say whether they wore blue or gray with all that gunsmoke hazing up the chill morning air. But a redbird, like they only grew back East, was chirping fit to bust above the rattle of small arms fire and occasional rumble of the field guns, so Long-arm knew where he was, now, and called out, "Stand your ground and fire back at 'em, boys! You'll just wind up with a bayonet up your ass if you run like raw recruits!"

"I'd rather have *this* in me!" a girlish voice replied as Private Custis Long from West-by-God Virginia insisted, "Let go my dong and fix your damn bayonet, boy!" Only to be coyly asked, "Do I feel like a *boy*, down here?" Which inspired him to move faster in her as he shook himself awake to mutter, "How did you get in here, Kim? That nice gal at the desk had orders to keep you away from me this trip!"

She hugged his bare hips with her naked thighs and dug her nails into his bounding buttocks as she moaned, "That nice gal behind the desk got off at midnight and she just knew no gal as beautiful and rich as the Widow Stover would want to mess with a gent of *our* social position unless he really knew how to treat a gal right and, oh, shit, you've already got me coming, you mean thing!"

Her delicately phrased orgasm inspired him to respond in kind and that, of course, woke him up all the way.

He didn't find it too disappointing, staring down at her in the dim light from the streetlamp out front as he got down to doing it right, now that he knew what he was doing.

For old Ben Franklin had been right about trees wilting from the top, and since her face was still reasonably pretty that allowed her to be downright lovely farther down, as far as he could see, at any rate. For while she seemed to have notions on free loving fit to shock the most advanced suf-fragette, she betrayed her middle-class upbringing by crawling into a gent's bed in her infernal satin shimmy shirt.

He said as much when she protested his shucking her out of it to nibble her naked nipples. She agreed it felt ever so much low-down and dirty, hence exciting to her, but asked if he didn't think they were screwing sort of trashy, even as she hugged his hairy bare chest closer to her firm and turgid tits. He assured her the head docs over to Vienna had written in officious books that only the very poor and very rich seemed to know how to let themselves go in bed together.

She giggled and asked how even a head doc might know what rich folk did to one another between silk sheets. He spread her thighs to a more conversational angle and replied, "I reckon anyone loco enough to go to a head doc with such problems to begin with would be likely to brag on 'em a mite. It stands to reason nobody would buy silk sheets to begin with unless they meant to get between 'em bare as I have you right now, bless your slithery hide."

She told him he was just awful and begged for him to slither all over her. So he did, and she did, but when they finally had to stop a spell and he lit a smoke for them to share, she coyly covered her privates with her hands and protested, "Oh, you mustn't look at me when I'm naked!"

He shook out the match, wondering just how he could go about informing such a shrinking violet of forty or so that he had to take a leak when he didn't even know her name or where the hotel crapper was. He was still working on that, his back teeth floating no matter how fast he smoked, when she solved the delicate social dilemma by sitting up and saying, "Turn your head the other way, dear. I have to use the potty."

He chuckled fondly and murmured, "Ladies first," as he blew smoke at the tin ceiling and she slid off the mattress to hunker down and hiss sedately into the mighty handy accommodation she'd hauled out from under the bedsprings.

He could tell she'd been considering the call to nature long before she'd given into it when, having farted as well, she suddenly jumped up to dash for the corner washstand, sobbing, "Oh, whatever must you think of me?"

To which he replied with a gallant chuckle, "That we're both human, of course. I'd feel dumb as hell coming in a supernatural being with parts just meant for show."

Suiting actions to words he swung his bare feet to the rug, bent over to pick up the chamber pot, and rose to contribute his own contents to it as she giggled girlishly in the far corner.

Thus it came to pass that when the door popped open and a sawed-off shotgun blasted their bed to a blizzard of feathers, neither Longarm nor the gal were in said bed. So the son of a bitch with the shotgun got to look even dumber when Longarm sloshed at least a quart of warm piss in his face and then busted the pot over his wet head.

It wasn't enough to drop the would-be assassin, albeit from the way he carried on, running off, he must have felt mighty chagrined. Longarm chased after him, despite his bare feet and ass, for the six-gun he grabbed from the bedpost on his way out the door was all that really counted if ever he got a halfway decent look at the bastard.

But he never. As he hit the bottom steps to materialize in all his naked glory in the lamp-lit lobby, the male night clerk behind the desk gasped, "He went thataway, and have you gone loco en la cabeza? You can't tear-ass about in public without even a fig leaf to your name! Who was that other lunatic and what was all that noise about just now?"

Longarm lowered his six-gun. There wasn't anything he could do about his dangling manhood that wouldn't make him look even dumber. So he contented himself with asking what the other one might have looked like. The night clerk replied without hesitation, "Wet. After that he was dark of duds and complexion. Gave the overall impression of a somewhat weathered cowhand and . . . Wait, he had on a pair of those laced-up boots, like some prospectors wear."

"Or sheepherders," Longarm muttered, half to himself. He took another step toward the front entrance, reconsidered, and told the night man he'd be up in his room and a mite more dressed for company when the law responded to that recent gunplay.

When he got upstairs neither the naked lady clerk nor her duds were anywhere to be seen. He leaped lightly over the busted china littering the soggy floor to either side of the doorjamb and kicked the door shut with a bare heel, muttering, "You'd think a gal prone to creep about the halls in search of late-night loving would learn to leave the door locked after her, at least." It was just now beginning to strike him that the shotgun sneak had caught *him* thinking more with his balls than his brains. As he got dressed he gripped his cheroot in bared teeth to growl, "That was really smart. You just came from locking up one gunslick someone sent after you and you came close to getting blasted out of bed behind a damned door you didn't even think to check!"

He'd just grumped on his boots and buckled the gun rig around his hips when there came a knock upon the now-locked door. Thinking it might be Dodge Preston or at least some of his deputies, Longarm trimmed the lamp again and opened the door again. When he saw it was a young Indian gal in a threadbare maid's outfit he put his gun away and opened wider to ask what he could do. She told him Miss Marge had told her to clean up after the "accident" they could both still see all over the flooring at their feet. He'd wondered if that older gal who screwed so fine had a name to go with her friendly ways. He told the younger but not as pretty chambermaid to go ahead, but felt obliged to add, "It wasn't exactly an accident. If you heard that ten gauge going off you'll no doubt be able to grasp why I done it on purpose."

She answered with the agreeable albeit noncommittal noises one uses on armed and possibly dangerous white men at such times until she stepped into the room with her bucket and wet mop to regard the results of number-nine buck on a feather mattress. Noting her wide-eyed concern Longarm

110

soothed, "You should have seen it in here before the feathers settled."

She asked if Miss Marge knew how bad things really were. He could have assured her Marge had to. But that wouldn't have been a favor to either of them. So he just said he wasn't sure because he'd run after the rascal, leaving the door ajar a spell. Before she could probe the mystery further Dodge Preston and two of his town deputies clumped in to join them. Preston sniffed, sighed, and said, "Old Walt behind the desk downstairs described the soggy shotgun toter to us. You sure are a hard man to kill, Longarm, when one considers how many hired guns you seem to have out to kill you!"

Longarm shrugged and said, "You might be answering your own question, Dodge. A man can only be so good, or so lucky, against the real thing. I suspect the not-too-bright bastard behind all this has recruited bush-league bad boys to do a man's job. The one as tried to back-shoot me in Thayer Junction messed up. The one you have on ice in your lockup talked too big for an experienced shootist, and neither of 'em seem at all well known. The only hardcases I've met up this way with Wanted papers posted on 'em were the two at the Smithfield spread, and they were out to give the Widow Smithfield a hard time. They hadn't been sent after me and—"

"Sandy MacPherson ain't with us no more," Preston cut in, morosely. Before Longarm could ask how come the disgusted local lawman explained, "Lawyer Spitzer came by with a writ of hocus-pocus less than an hour ago. I just heard and so I was wondering whether I ought to wake you up about it when it transpired to all within earshot that you were awake indeed."

Longarm swore and said, "We've got to get that young fool back before they do him in to shut him up! Do you know where to find that tinhorn lawyer, sudden?"

Preston nodded but said, "It won't do no good. We call him Spitzer the Shitzer and that's a compliment, once you

111

know him. I've already been to see Spitzer. He said I was welcome to look under the house for the kid without a search warrant, meaning he was likely telling the truth about the late or soon-to-be-late Sandy MacPherson not being on the premises. When I asked who paid him to spring the dumb little shit he naturally told me that was lawyer-client and hence private information. Do you reckon he could make that stick if we was to run him in?''

Longarm nodded soberly and said, ''Take it from one who knows and never try to arrest a lawyer who can get a judge to sign a writ of habeas corpus after suppertime.''

Preston stared morosely at the maid cleaning up after the latest attempt on Longarm's life as he bleakly observed, ''You know that if we can't get that courthouse toady to tell us who hired him, we'll just never know what ever happened to Sandy MacPherson, don't you?''

To which Longarm replied, as cheerfully, ''Don't be such a pessimist, pard. They may not bother hiding his body all that mysterious, once they make sure he's in no shape to tell us shit.''

Chapter 9

Lawyer Spitzer apparently felt it wiser to dwell upwind of the cow town's business district, but he ran his stinky law practice from a second-story office above a saloon near the courthouse.

Longarm wasn't sure an early-morning visit was worth his time as he strode up the shady side of the street. He knew it couldn't be worth it when he spied the brand on a side-saddled bay tethered to the rail of the steps running up the side of the building to the offices above.

Kim Stover had taken to riding mighty fancy since she'd started breeding up her beef herd with whiteface stock and attending fancy balls in Cheyenne and Chicago. But even in her more natural days, when first they'd met, Kim had been too refined to drink in broad day in a public saloon, since ladies were not considered part of the public when it came to saloons, or behaving like ladies. There was a dentist's office up on that second floor, according to gilt letters in one window. As he stood in the shade of a feed store across the way, lighting a cheroot as an excuse to cover his own face, he hoped old Kim had a toothache. For everyone he'd asked had assured him Lawyer Spitzer was slippery as an eel and crooked as a split rail fence. Kim Stover, for all her money and other faults, had never lied to Longarm or anyone else, as far as he knew. That was one of the things that made him anxious to avoid her. For not going to bed with Kim Stover, once they locked eyes, was as likely as the sun not setting once the day was done, only, damn it, she'd never learned that an ounce of white lies beat a ton of explanations, and it sure did take the edge off romance to have a female call you a damned old Don Juan even before you'd finished Don Juaning her right. So he stood there just smoking some. Then, when it commenced to become obvious that she was up there to stay a spell he eased back down to the livery to skin the cat another way.

He hadn't expected Lawyer Spitzer to level with him, and Billy Vail hadn't sent him all this way to jaw with small-town lawyers about two-bit gun waddies to begin with. He had the day crew at the livery get the buckskin out, and after they'd saddled her up he shoved his Winchester in the saddle boot, mounted up, and rode out of town to the north via a back alley Kim Stover had no likely reason to ride through.

For the official mailing address of the mysterious L. J. Travis lay between Honeycomb and the hills dividing the Red Desert from the watershed of the eastbound Sweetwater. Whether the would-be monarch of the Wyoming mutton industry would be there to accept the writ from the BLM or not, there had to be someone at his home spread with some notion where the hell he really was and, better yet, Longarm knew anyone trying to keep him from serving said writ would have a chore tailing him unseen across the open sage flats between Honeycomb and the Travis spread.

It was sort of disappointing to notice, once he'd ridden well out of sight of town, that nobody seemed to be tailing him. It was easy enough to glance back now and again without being obvious. The big sky above and all around was a cloudless cobalt dome. The late morning sun dazzled down on dead-still silvery sage tips, since there wasn't a breath of wind. The only slight disturbance for miles seemed occasioned by a flock of carrion crows hovering a quarter mile out to the west of the wagon trace, cussing in crow caws at something down in the sage below them. Longarm patted the neck of his slightly spooked pony to say, soothingly, "Keep going and thank Wakan Tonka the west wind ain't blowing. There wouldn't be such a fuss if Old Man Coyote was guarding a rabbit from them flying flesh eaters. Range wolves likely pulled down a half-grown cow or full-grown sheep during the night. Crows would have found it first if it had just up and died."

He lit another smoke, more to comfort the keener nostrils of his pony than because of any need for nicotine right now. Ponies just hated the faintest scent of death and . . .

"When you're spooked you're spooked," he decided, reining in and dismounting to tether the buckskin to a sage brush and haul the Winchester out of its boot. "I'll be back directly and we'll have a good laugh about a sheep kill spooking you from so far off with the air barely moving."

Then he started walking toward the hovering cloud of crows, a mite spooked himself. For he knew that the buckskin was a trained cow pony that just shouldn't have been that proddy about dead stock. So what did that leave the buckskin to feel proddy about?

There were four wolves, for openers. Three ran off as soon as they spied Longarm striding tall at them through the sage with a long gun cradled over an elbow. The boss wolf, she looked to have some Indian dog blood in her, stood her ground and growled at him like one of her more domesticated ancestors guarding a Shoshone baby. Only that wasn't what she was trying to keep Longarm from getting to. As he spied the spurred Justins peeking coyly at him from around a sage clump Longarm shifted the Winchester to a more businesslike position and told the tough old bitch-wolf, "You'll find me a live-and-let-live cuss up to a point, ma'am. But don't push it, hear?"

The wolf understood his tone, if not the words, and slowly slunk aside, half growling and half whining as he soothed, "I know you and your kids didn't do it. But I still can't let you eat the evidence."

He took a deep breath and eased around the clump for a better view. He still had a time not puking his breakfast entire, for however Sandy MacPherson had been killed, the wolves had started with his exposed face and temptingly scented crotch.

The body lay spread-eagled on its back, the bandaged hands protected by the medicinal odor of the burn dressings as much as by the bandages. For as anyone could see by regarding the pants of the mutilated cadaver, once a hungry wolf decided to nibble something it got nibbled indeed.

Longarm glared down at the dead boy, almost biting through the cheroot gripped in his bared teeth, as he growled, "Now you've done it, you silly son of a bitch! How in thunder am I supposed to serve the damed writ on that damned sheepherder if you assholes keep getting in my way?"

Sandy MacPherson offered no comment on the matter as Longarm had to hunker down and grab one booted ankle, muttering, "All right, come along little darling and thank your stars I tied that pony good. For I ain't about to haul you all the way back to town, myself, and unless someone does, those crows will peck away all of you those damed wolves leave."

The corpse had gone stiff enough to drag fairly handy across the dust and thatch between the sage clumps. It still seemed one hell of a ways, and when they got close enough to matter the buckskin commenced rolling her eyes and fighting the bit to put some distance between herself and the dead boy.

Longarm knew it was the smell of human blood that

bothered her most. MacPherson hadn't been dead long enough to stink in the cool dry air of the Red Desert. Cavalry horses were broken in by letting them smell gunsmoke and rotten meat ahead of time. They still tended to bolt the first time they scented *human* blood, and naturally cow ponies weren't as likely to.

So to say Longarm had a time packing the mortal remains of Sandy MacPherson back to Honeycomb, facedown across the McClellan as its usual rider had to walk all the way, was to say that digging postholes in adobe dirt with a spoon was an easy chore. By the time Longarm had the silly son of a bitch back to town and propped up on a cellar door for the doc to look over, he was certain he'd have rather dug those postholes, in solid rock, with his infernal fingernails. The doc said Sandy MacPherson had been shot in the back. Longarm wasn't at all surprised.

To judge by the way everyone carried on, one would have thought a partly eaten corpse was a novelty in Honeycomb Township. What with one damned thing and another it was well past noon when Longarm tried Lawyer Spitzer's office again and, finding Kim Stover's pony no longer there, went on up to ask some serious questions about the boy Spitzer had sprung from the town lockup less than thirteen unfortunate hours before.

But when he entered the reception room behind the frosty glass door with SILAS SPITZER ESQUIRE lettered on it in black, he found himself facing down a sort of pretty but unpleasantly plump young gal with light brown hair that sort of clashed with her rust-red summer dress. He flashed his badge and I.D. at her and said he'd like a word with her employer, boyfriend or whatever. She blushed and confided she had no boyfriend and that her boss hadn't come in yet. He hauled out his pocket watch and consulted it before he asked how come, adding, "It's almost one o'clock, and didn't a client answering to Kim Stover have an earlier appointment with him? I'd like you to study some before you answer that,

117

Miss. We're going to get along lots better if we don't start out fibbing.''

The not-too-bright-looking secretary looked sincerely puzzled as she told him, ''I don't know why you think anyone's fibbing to you, sir. Miss Kim just left less than fifteen minutes ago. Are you anxious to catch up with her, too?''

Longarm shook his head and said, ''Already jawed all I want with her.'' Which was the simple truth if one wanted to study on the last time he'd been in the feathers with the teary eyed little thing. He asked the more cheerful looking fat gal, ''How could Kim Stover have come and gone if your boss hasn't been in at all, Miss, ah . . . ?''

''Poppy, Poppy Jane Kraus,'' she replied, as if she had a right to be proud about that. Then she explained, ''Miss Kim was by to pick up some papers we'd already prepared for her. So she didn't have to see Mr. Silas. So there.''

He smiled down sheepishly and replied, ''I stand corrected. Since you do his typing, might you be able to tell me anything about a writ of habeas corpus served on Marshal Preston late last night?''

She looked sincerely innocent as she replied, ''I fear I can't tell you anything about it. I haven't seen Mr. Silas since he left here yesterday afternoon. Who was the judge who issued the writ? He or his own stenographer would surely know more about it than I.''

Longarm started to haul out his notebook. Then he decided, ''I have a writ of my own to worry about and this sidetracking sure is getting tedious. So let's try her another way. You say your boss has been working for Miss Kim Stover? No offense, but I happen to know she retains the services of a somewhat bigger Cheyenne law firm.''

The fat gal working in the much more modest Honeycomb office nodded and replied, ''That she does indeed. She has a fancy law firm on retainer in Chicago as well. What with her own mining, lumber, and stock spread all about the country her affairs are more than one law firm could properly ride herd on. All we handle for her is her stock insurance, in this particular corner of Wyoming Territory, that is. We have nothing to say about her herds up along the Peace River in Canada.''

Longarm frowned and said, ''Say something about her mutton and beef between here and Bitter Creek, then. She never mentioned insuring cows or sheep, for Pete's sake, when last we, ah, met.''

Poppy Jane nodded knowingly and replied, ''It's not easy coverage to get, what with wolves, the Red Sash Gang and all. We're the only firm in these parts offering stock insurance at all.''

Considering Lawyer Spitzer's reputation and Kim Stover's honesty, Longarm found the part about insurance easy to believe. He had a time swallowing the part about red sashes, though. He smiled thinly and said, ''I keep hearing about the Red Sash Gang. For some reason neither I nor any other lawman I know seems to have seen any such dramatic cow thieves. I take it Lawyer Spitzer hasn't had to pay out all that much on stock run off by such pests?''

She rapped her pudgy knuckles on the wooden edge of her desk as she replied, ''Our clients have been luckier than some. Mr. Silas doesn't insure anything direct, by the way. We only act as local agents for Universal Underwriters of Omaha. You've heard of them, of course?''

Longarm said, ''No, but I sure mean to. You just said nobody insuring stock with you has suffered many losses. Might that be your way of saying others in these parts have?''

She said she'd heard the Red Sash Gang had been behaving just awful since they'd drifted down this way from the Powder River range, but that of course they kept no records of stockmen they hadn't sold any insurance to, as yet.

He said, ''I want you to study on this next question and if you feel you can't answer it, just say so, without fibbing.''

He waited for her to nod and then asked, ''Does a big

sheepman called L. J. Travis have his stock insured by you, Miss Poppy Jane?''

She looked him smack in the eye as she replied without much apparent thought, ''No. I can tell you without looking it up that nobody has insured any sheep with us. The Red Sash Gang has run off many a head of beef but, so far and knock wood, no mutton at all.''

He asked, ''What about Kim Stover, then?''

''Not her sheep, her cows, silly! Didn't you know she's about the biggest cattle baroness there ever was?''

He didn't want to talk about other gals who seemed to think they were cowboys since that infernal Virginia Wood-hull had taken to writing all that fuss and feathers about women's rights. So he just nodded and said, ''Long as I'm here, I'd like to take down a list of all the cow outfits you've insured so far.''

It didn't work. She went on smiling, but her plump little jaw set sort of stubborn as she replied, ''I couldn't let you go through our confidential office records, sir. Not without a court order, ah, if you'd like to see if you can get one.''

He sighed and asked if she'd rather he built her a snowman out front. When she laughed and said, ''Silly, it's the middle of high summer!'' he nodded and said that was what he'd meant. Then he told her he'd be back sometime when her boss was in. She said she'd tell Lawyer Spitzer he'd been by. That left him nothing more sensible to say to her, so he left.

There was enough of the day left to resume his busted-off ride out to the Travis spread. So he walked back to where he'd left his buckskin in the shade, near the cellar door they'd propped young Sandy MacPherson up on, in case anyone in town had anything to add to his sad story.

There was still a modest crowd around the mutilated remains. Longarm had already seen them, so he didn't look too close as he got back aboard the buckskin and started to ride on. Then he reined in, dismounted, and bulled his way through the crowd for a closer gander, muttering, ''What the hell and when in hell?'' For he'd been right about that flash of sunlit scarlet he'd glimpsed through the confusion around the corpse.

Some silly son of a bitch had tied a sash of bright red silk around the dead boy's waist and when Longarm asked, nobody there could tell him who, or why. It just sounded stupid when a young cowhand opined, ''They say he started a fight with a U.S. marshal just last night. So it stands to reason he was an outlaw, and that red sash tells us clear enough what gang he was riding with, see?''

Chapter 10

Longarm availed himself of the services of Western Union before heading out once more for the Travis spread with the land office writ in a hip pocket and his Winchester cocked across the saddle swells.

This time he made it almost all the way without incident. When at last he spied the twin sunflower windmills he'd been told to watch for, off to the east of the South Pass City wagon trace, the incidents commenced poco tiempo.

As he rode in across range not as badly overgrazed as he'd been expecting to see, he saw two ragged riders and a brace of barking sheepdogs herding at least two hundred head of sheep toward the same windmills, albeit from the southeast as he rode in from the southwest. Spying sheep on or about a sheep spread seemed reasonable and the one sheepdog that cut between him and the herd, snapping and snarling fit to bust, was only doing its job.

The trio of riders bearing down on Longarm from the direction of the twin windmills looked more ominous. All three packed long guns of their own, and not as politely as Longarm. So as they came within easy rifle range Longarm reined in, dismounted, and moved clear of his buckskin with his Winchester pointed just as unfriendly.

His no-bullshit move inspired the mounted sheepman in the middle to raise one hand as if he thought he was a cavalry leader and move closer on his own after halting his sidekicks. His saddle gun's muzzle drooped at a more polite angle when he next reined in at easy pistol range to call out, as firmly as politely, "You're on private property, cowboy. Why don't you just get back on that buckskin and get both your asses back on the wagon trace before either of 'em suffer mortal harm?"

Longarm replied as certainly, "I mean to do just that, after I've paid me a formal call on L. J. Travis at the home spread claimed in the very same name."

"The boss ain't to home," the mounted rifleman barring his path replied.

"In that case any close kin or, hell, his ramrod or house-keeper will do."

"We're not empowered to entertain visitors when the boss ain't to home," the sheepman insisted.

So Longarm insisted, "That's all right. I'm neither a visitor nor a lonesome cowboy. I'm the law, federal, and if push comes to shove I can always call on a troop of dragoons from Fort Fred Steele to gently tap upon the door for me."

"Do you have a search warrant?" the sheepman stubbornly tried.

Longarm sighed wearily and told him, "I reckon I could get one in the time it'll take the boys in blue to ride all the way up from that outpost along the railroad tracks. Do I really have to tell you how thorough we're likely to search your whole fucking spread if and when you put us to that much trouble?"

The sheepman must have been able to guess. But he blustered, "See here, we've got nothing to hide out here!"

Longarm smiled sweetly and said, "Bueno. In that case we got nothing to argue about and so what are we arguing about?" Then he got back aboard his buckskin to add, "Lead on, MacDuff, or would you rather I called you something closer to what your mama named you?"

The surly sheepman growled, "You can call me Ramon Eskabal and you'd best leave my mama out of it. They ain't going to like this, up to the big house, but they'd likely fuss at us for gunning a government man, too, so let's go."

They went, the leader saying something to his followers in a lingo Longarm had heard before but couldn't even try to savvy. Ramon and the other two were wiry gents with olive complexions and fine-boned skulls. Longarm had not the least notion why so many Basques from the peaks between old Spain and France had come all the way out to the American West to take up sheepherding. But he didn't see what else Ramon and his compatriots could be. From the way he talked plain American, Ramon had been on this side of the pond most of his adult life. You had to take up a new lingo before puberty to speak it without a trace of accent. Longarm didn't suspect Ramon would take it as a compliment if someone told him he didn't sound as dago as he looked, so why say it?

It seemed wiser to comment on the herd of sheep as they rode past it, sheep not being noted for fleetness of foot. When Longarm asked how many head they grazed smack on the home spread itself, Ramon said, "They don't belong to Don Travis. We were asked to help out a herder working for the Widow Stover, a business associate and family friend. She had none of her own people working the range as close to the Tanglewaters as we are."

There were times to show how smart you were and there were times it was smart to act dumb. Not knowing which might be best at the moment, Longarm tried, "I heard in town that a Stover herder called Shorty had been stranded with no dog and a scattered herd."

Ramon pointed back at the woolly-backs with his braided

leather riding quirt to say, "You heard right. Those are the sheep we're talking about and they were scattered from hell to breakfast. The sons of bitches who shot Shorty Blare's sheepdog must have come back, later. Poor old Shorty lay sort of scattered as well. Funny how wolves would rather worry something already dead than go to the trouble of pulling down fresh meat."

Longarm stared thundergasted as Ramon's grim words sunk in. He asked for more details. Ramon shrugged and said, "I wasn't there. Jim Baxter, one of the hands we sent south with supplies and spare hounds for Shorty, rode in ahead of the herd and those other boys we just passed. He'll be at the house, if they let you in and Jim thinks it's any of your business."

Longarm didn't waste time arguing that point with a man who really had little say in the matter. They topped a slight rise to see the low-slung sprawl of tin-roofed soddies between the twin windmills and the Antelope Hills running east-west cross-grain along the northern horizon. One windmill fed a big shallow stock tank, half in the dooryard and half fenced into one corner of a big corral, empty save a couple of ponies and a goat, at the moment.

The other windmill fed a smaller but higher tank that seemed to feed running water to the main house and outbuildings. There were fair-sized windows glazed with real glass along the south-facing front wall of the long low house. So old L. J. Travis had been making out pretty well, grazing his infernal sheep on Uncle Sam's sage, and you'd think the son of a bitch would feel patriotic enough to pay for it. Washington favored western settlement to the point where rural whites back East as well as Indians out west were inclined to bitch, with some justification. It wasn't as if the Bureau of Land Management overcharged or, hell, charged a sensible price for the natural resources they encouraged anyone half white to exploit out this way. Thinking about that reminded Longarm of the now somewhat wilted writ he was packing for the range hog. It would have been tempting to just slip it to Ramon or anyone else who might have been left in charge out here. A lot of process servers were inclined to let it go at that. A lot of scofflaws with slick lawyers were inclined to claim, later, that they hadn't been properly served, when one came to study on it.

So when a pretty gal wearing a sort of fandango skirt and a darker complexion than her Basque riders came out on the veranda to fuss at them for letting Longarm near her, then admit she was in fact the lady of the house, Longarm dismounted with both his Winchester and the government writ put away, for now.

Once the pretty little thing had been made to understand what a stubborn cuss Longarm could be about trespassing on posted property, she relented enough to grudgingly invite him in for some coffee, at least, and added as Longarm and Ramon followed her that she could deal with the damned old government for L. J. Travis because she was his only child, Belinda.

Longarm was too polite to say he was glad to see the old gent he'd come to pester was a doting daddy instead of a dirty old man. As she clapped her hands and indicated seats by the cold fireplace she asked Longarm just what Uncle Sam wanted from her dear old dad.

Longarm had to wait until a Shoshone gal in a maid's livery came out from the back to take Miss Belinda's orders to the Chinese cook. Ramon cut in to protest, "Nothing for me, Miss Belinda, I have to oversee those Stover sheep coming in. You'll want 'em held in the main corral until Kim Stover sends her own boys for 'em, right?"

She told him he was on the money in such a dimpling way that Longarm suspected old Ramon treated her right in other ways, given half the chance. As Ramon left she told Longarm her father might not be in off the range this side of fall sell-off, so, right, Ramon had more than half a chance.

That wasn't what he'd come all this way to investigate, however, so as the maid spread coffee and shortbread on the low-slung table between their two armchairs Longarm told Belinda Travis about the beef the BLM had with her dad about his sheep and she didn't seem to understand when he told her she couldn't have the writ, herself. He said, "They already sent one process server out here to haul your dad into court as a range hog, no offense, and he never came back."

She answered, "Pooh!" and poured for both of them as she went on, "Marshal Preston was out here asking about that priss. I told him what I'm telling you right now. We never saw hide nor hair of him. Before you ask what might have happened to him, we just don't know. It was early spring, with a couple of blizzards left in the air on the mostly empty Red Desert. Riders who know the high country wind up vanished forever more on the Red Desert. Don't ever get blown off your mount by wolf winds left over from our long winters if you don't fancy being eaten by wolves. Real ones."

He bit into some shortbread and said, "I met one just this morning that looked part dog. By the way, do you know a young cowhand called Sandy MacPherson?"

She wrinkled her nose in what seemed genuine distaste before she replied, "My father would disown me if I knew a cowhand by any name or description. They have no sensible reason to be on or about the Red Desert, and who'd want to associate with senseless folk?"

He washed down some shortbread with coffee and dryly asked, "Was Ramon fibbing when he said you were on good terms with Kim Stover, the cattle queen of Wyoming?"

It didn't faze her. She answered easily, "Kim's not senseless. She's about as smart a human being as I know, male or female. She keeps her cows and cowhands up on the Wind River range, where cows and cowhands belong. She only grazes sheep down here on the sage flats, knowing sheep from cattle country."

He nodded soberly and said, "Old Kim digs coal up

Sheridan way as well. I can see why she'd call on you folk when she got word one of her sheepherders needed a helping hand. I'd like a few words with your boy about what they found down by the Tanglewaters before I leave. But first things coming first, let's study on where your dad might be right now, Miss Belinda.''

She turned a duskier shade of rose and looked away as she said, ''I've already told you. Dad's out on the range somewhere. Why can't you just serve your papers on me and I'll get a lawyer to answer for us in court.''

Longarm shook his head and said, ''The government don't want a lawyer showing up to ask for a delay until the sweet by-and-by, Miss Belinda. They've been trying to settle up with your dad since they found out last fall about his overgrazing.''

She shook her head a mite wild eyed and snapped, ''We never! No matter who told you we were overstocking they were lying. Does my poor father look like a petty crook to you?''

He chuckled despite himself and replied, ''I wouldn't know him if he walked in right now to catch us kissing, and if it's all no more than a mathematical misunderstanding, why won't you just tell me where in thunder he might be so I can just serve him the infernal writ and he can straighten it out with the infernal BLM?''

She started to say something about how vast the Red Desert was. Then she shot him an arch look and asked, ''Hold on, might you by any chance be the Deputy Long some call Longarm?''

He honestly had to allow some called him worse things than that. When he asked her what had made her suspect his nickname she blushed even rosier and confided, ''Kim Stover told me what you looked like and said you were inclined to make fresh remarks without really meaning to sound so shocking.''

He started to ask when he'd ever said anything halfway fresh at her. Then he grinned sheepishly and said he hadn't

129

planned on her dear old dad catching them in the act of anything all that literal and cautiously added, "What else might old Kim have told you about my scandalous habits, Miss Belinda?"

"She made me promise I'd never repeat some of the more shocking parts. My point is that she also told me you're a gentleman of the old school when it comes to keeping a lady's little secrets."

He nodded but felt obliged to warn her, "I'm still a lawman, sworn to uphold the Constitution of these United States, within reason. So you'd best study on that before you tell me any secrets, ma'am."

She fiddled absently with half-eaten shortbread, staring into the cooled ashes of her fireplace as if she expected to see something more interesting there. Then she decided, "Kim said you're too smart to fib to and I'm not certain whether I've broken any federal laws or not. Are we, ah, holding this conversation in private?"

He nodded soberly and said, "I don't see anyone else in here and my boss just hates it when it's just my word against that of a mighty pretty lady."

She smiled, albeit bitterly, and said, "Thanks for the gallantry but let's start with that. You've already noticed I'm a woman. One of my grandmothers on my father's side was of the darker persuasion and my mother was a Blackfoot squaw. So what would you say that made me in the eyes of the law?"

He didn't bat an eye. He said, "A pretty little gal with a mighty big chip on her shoulder, if you're asking about state laws, in some states. You could be refused certain privileges in some parts of the country if you went and blabbed about your, ah, suntan. Federal law ain't all that fussy and since it's still a territory Wyoming abides by mostly federal statutes. What did you have in mind, getting served strong liquor as someone with some Indian blood or marrying up with a purely white man as someone not quite so pure? By the way, are Basques considered white folk?"

She laughed despite herself and said, "Don't you ever dare ask Ramon a question like that. What he and I might be planning in the future is neither here nor there. Kim Stover tells me she had a time getting the property of her late husbands in her own name, free and clear, on account some mean old men said she was too female to manage her own property and—"

"She told me about that," he cut in. "Some idiots can't seem to savvy that women are allowed to own property in this country, even if they don't get to serve in wartime, vote, and so on. But just what property might we be talking about in connection with your own female persuasion, Miss Belinda?"

She made a sweeping gesture around the room with her shortbread and said, "All of this, along with sheep grazing out on the open range in any direction you'd care to point. To tell the honest truth I just don't know the full extent of my late father's estate. Kim Stover told me to tally everything on paper and let her take it to some lawyers she knows before we announce the death in the family, see?"

Longarm whistled softly and replied, "If you're saying the one and original L. J. Travis has up and *died* on us, intestate and without so much as a word from the county coroner . . . When did it happen and where might he be buried, illegal, right now?"

She told him bleakly, "Dad passed away last winter, natural, under this very roof. We buried him on the rise to the north. We had to, before the ground froze too stiff."

Longarm cocked an eyebrow to ask, "Without reporting it, even to the town law in Honeycomb?"

She sighed and said, "It sounds easier in high summer than it is in winter with the wolf winds blowing and the snow piled ten feet deep in places. I just told you my other reasons for sort of hesitating. When I wrote Kim Stover about it, this spring, she rode down from her spread instead of writing back. She said some things were best not put on paper. She seemed to share your view I'd been a mite hasty in planting my dead dad without a proper permit. She told me, meanwhile, to just keep quiet and let her law firm study on it some before we make anything official."

Longarm nodded soberly and said, "It's a good thing we never had this conversation, official, then. If I can't find the stockman this writ is made out to, I don't see how anyone can expect me to serve it on anyone. But, unofficial, what can you tell me about the charges your dad had way more stock grazing government range than he ever paid the fee for?"

She was either sincere or one hell of a liar, he felt sure, as she assured him, "Dad never would have done anything that cheap and stupid. The range fees for sheep are less than half as much as those for cows, and they only ask a few cents a head for cows! You can see for yourself what a sizable operation my poor old dad built up out here on the Red Desert. Why would anyone with half a brain risk it all to cheat the BLM out of a few pennies?"

He finished his coffee and leaned back, saying, "Pennies add up, when you put enough critters out on the taxpayers pasturage, and no offense, your dad's figures failed to match those of the BLM. Call 'em nitpickers if you will, Miss Belinda, but the pencil pushers keeping books for Uncle Sam have no call to fib about the figures."

Her lower lip quivered and she looked so hurt he felt obliged to try, "You say he died natural last winter. That means he might have been feeling poorly last fall when he was selling stock, paying off his grazing fees and so forth. So, look, I never had orders to arrest nobody as a range hog. The writ I'm packing is a simple show-cause order. Owning up to some sloppy figures and offering to pay the extra grazing costs along with penalties and interest ought to get you off the hook, see?"

She said she did and asked for the writ so she could get the dumb business out of the way. He shook his head and told her, "It's not made out in your name and it's best to eat the apple one bite at a time, Miss Belinda. I just told

132

you how I can buy some time for you by simply failing to
find your dad anywhere in these parts. Meanwhile you and
Kim, or Kim's law firm, better nail down your clear title
to all your dad's property and livestock. You'd feel mighty
silly paying off your dad's just debts only to find out someone else held title to his estate.''

She looked stricken, but said, ''I'm his only living re-
lation and dear Kim will be riding out here anytime now.
She was planning on spending the night out here after fin-
ishing her business in Honeycomb.''

It was Longarm's turn to look stricken, but he tried not
to as he glanced out the nearest window, saw how long the
afternoon shadows were getting, and got to his feet, saying,
''I'm sure you gals will have a lot to talk about. Meanwhile
I'd best have a word with your hands about the death of
Kim's sheepherder, Shorty Blare. For he was alive and well
when last we parted friendly, and if he was killed on federal
range my boss is going to want a full report, in triplicate,
whether we ever find out who done it or not.''

She followed him to the door, asking if he didn't want
to stay and enjoy supper with Kim Stover, once she showed
up. He said he just hated the notion of missing a sit-down
supper with his old pal Kim, but that he had to get cracking.
It wouldn't have been nice to say what else he'd likely wind
up enjoying if he didn't get out of here before that tempting
as well as tempted blonde hove into view. He knew that,
deep down, he was doing both himself and old Kim a favor
by not starting up with her again. For he, and likely she,
could handle bittersweet romances best when they didn't
end so bitter, and there was just no way a man could get
out of bed after bedding Kim Stover that didn't hurt bitter
as bile!

Out in the dooryard, where he could see the sun even
better, he saw he'd best get it on down the road if he meant
to avoid Kim trapping him out here. But while a man had
to think of the feelings of himself and his friends, he had
to put his duty first, and there was simply no way a self-

respecting lawman could ride off without word-one about that poor young sheepherder's killing. For they'd shook and parted friendly, with Longarm promising to get help to the bewhiskered youth and, damn it, someone had jumped him and fed him to the wolves before help had ever arrived.

As he spied Ramon talking to other hands over by the well-stocked corral, he muttered, "Damn it to hell. The case I was sent on seems stupidly simple. So how come I got all these other side killings to study on?"

The sheepherders who'd brought back the Stover herd after finding Shorty Blare dead as well as dogless were little help, even with Longarm taking notes and backing them over some questions. Jim Baxter, the one who'd found the body and ridden back ahead of the sheep with the news, was a young, fairly bright looking colored gent who, when asked, said he was certain the body they'd found had been that of Shorty Blare. He said, "I knew Mr. Shorty well. He backed me against some mean white cowboys in Honeycomb one time."

Longarm agreed the gent he'd met farther south had seemed a decent cuss but thought he'd better point out, "I left a cuss dressed more cow sort of spread out for the wolves down yonder."

That cost him the time it took to tell the whole tale of his shoot-out and track-down to the bemused sheepherders, and the infernal sun was getting lower, not higher, all the while.

When he'd finished about finding the mounted back-shooter dead aboard that thoroughbred, near the marshy stretch, one of the others who'd ridden down that way with Baxter said, "We never saw anyone but Shorty down yonder, dead or alive. We never poked about in marsh reeds for bodies we had no reason to consider. We all knew Shorty Blare on sight and it's a good thing, too. The damned crows had took his eyes and the damned wolves had gnawed the rest of him considerable!"

"It was Mr. Shorty," Jim Baxter insisted. "I don't see

why even the Red Sash Gang would want to do in such a quality gent. The Stover sheep had scattered all about, but none was down or missing entire and they hadn't even looted Mr. Shorty's wagon, as far as we could tell.''

Longarm asked about the young sheepherder's pony and established it was missing, along with Blare's shotgun and side arms he might have had. Longarm grimaced and said, ''Men caught alone on the range have been killed for their pony and guns before. Run that part about the Red Sash Gang by me some more. The way I hear it, those Powder River toughs haven't been pestering any sheep outfits, even if one assumes they really exist.''

Jim Baxter said, ''Oh, they exist, sure enough. More than one cowhand has accused us sheepmen of aiding and abetting the Red Sash Gang.''

Another sheepherder nodded and chimed in with, ''Cowboys talk dumb as cows. Why would outlaws who speculate in stealing cows hide out on sheep spreads?''

The question was too dumb to bother answering and Longarm was as willing to believe in the tooth fairy as the Red Sash Gang in any case. So he just asked if they'd heard anything about that big insurance company offering coverage to anyone in the mutton industry, and when they just laughed he mounted up to haul ass before Kim Stover could catch him out here with his pants up.

Chapter 11

It was early but well after sundown when Longarm rode into town, tipped the livery crew extra to rub the buckskin down good before they watered and fed her, and then fed himself at a stand-up hole-in-the-wall serving pretty fair coffee and even better hot tamales cooked in corn husks and served wrapped in newspaper. It reminded Longarm of the old Mex who served the same, about as good, from his pushcart at Colfax and Broadway, down in Denver.

Thinking about Denver inspired him to think of all the far less complicated females who'd likely be sleeping alone down yonder this very evening, bless their poor frustrated hides.

Another widow woman he knew on Sherman Avenue was almost as slender waisted and wriggle hipped as old Kim, albeit not quite as young, while Miss Morgana Floyd out Arvada way and that redhead who served suds until midnight at the Black Cat were less apt to cry and tell a man he'd never really loved 'em once he'd loved all anyone sensible could stand in one night.

As he topped off his quick bite with more coffee and a slab of sweet Mexican pastry Longarm warned himself not to daydream his fool pecker hard so early on a likely lonesome night. As he strode off into the gathering gloom he growled, half aloud, "You could have stood out yonder at that sheep spread and likely wound up riding all the way home with old Kin Kim, you noble-ass nitwit. So let's stick to the business at hand and keep our damned hands off our poor pecker!"

The saloons and even some of the stores were still going full blast along Main Street, but if anything that made the shadows darker where lamplight didn't linger. So he felt pretty sure nobody was staring at him as he strode boldly up the outside steps of the noisy saloon under the dark deserted offices on the second floor.

Longarm's no doubt illegal but ever handy jackknife blade filed down by a Denver locksmith who should have been ashamed of himself made short work of the few locked doors he had to get through.

Going through the office files of Lawyer Spitzer took a lot more time. He didn't dare light the reading light on Spitzer's desk. The light coming in from outside made the reading tough as well as tedious.

Taking notes with his own stub pencil and some of Lawyer Spitzer's legal-sized notepaper so he'd have some grasp on what he was doing, Longarm confirmed that while nobody running sheep on the Red Desert seemed interested in insuring the same, Spitzer had peddled a surprising amount of stock insurance to cow outfits ranging between the Antelope Hills and Bitter Creek. He searched for signs of any claims paid out by the Omaha insurance outfit. When at last he found the right folder he saw Universal Underwriters had gotten off light, so far. A cow was certain to get struck by lightning here while a calf would get pulled down by wolves there, but he found no claims for serious losses. So what was all this bull about the Red Sash Gang coming down from the Powder River range to rob everyone blind?

He found a couple of claims on missing stock that could have been lost strayed or stolen. Poppy Jane had attached carbons of the letters Lawyer Spitzer had dictated in reply. Longarm chuckled and muttered, "They were right to dub him Spitzer the Shitzer." For naturally the wily cuss had advised them to read the small print on their policies.

Longarm had just about satisfied himself up there alone in the dark when the door opened and the plump Poppy Jane came in to strike a match and scream like a banshee when she spied Longarm behind her employer's desk. He moved quickly to wrap one strong arm around her soft torso and clap a hand over her wet mouth, soothing, "Simmer down, it's me!" Which inspired her to try and bite his hand off, whoever he might be.

Fortunately Longarm's palm was flat against her teeth as well as work hardened. When she saw she couldn't bite him hard enough to do her much good she went limp. So he had to let go of her face to hang on to her considerable mass with both arms and, as he did so, she moaned, "Oh, please be gentle with me, I'm a virgin, almost."

He tried not to laugh as he replied, "I don't doubt that, Miss Poppy Jane. But like I was saying, I'm the law, not the villain you seem to take me for."

She stared wide eyed up at him in the dim light, her match having winked out amid all the confusion, and gasped, "Oh, heavens above! What are you doing here, Deputy Long, and how did you ever get in?"

"The door was unlocked," he lied, knowing better than to tell a legal secretary he'd picked the doors without a search warrant. She seemed to accept this. So as he let go of her he asked if she was working late or getting to work mighty early. She told him, "Mr. Silas sent me over for some insurance forms."

He said, "I notice he's been insuring a heap of stock. You told me earlier he was missing from human ken and that he'd sold stock insurance to the Widow Stover. Would you like to change either story now?"

She looked blankly up at him, then said, "I told you he was out of the office on business. He's at home, right now, if you'd like me to take you to him. As for insuring Miss Kim's stock, you'll have to ask him, or her. All I know is that she came by, asking for him, and when I said he wasn't in and asked how come she said something about stock insurance and left, not long before you came in, as a matter of fact."

He decided to buy her words at face value, but said, "Kim Stover doesn't have any beef this far south and nobody seems anxious to insure mutton. I don't suppose you could tell me why?"

She shrugged her plump shoulders and said she had no idea, adding he could ask Lawyer Spitzer, who might know more than she did about such matters.

He grimaced and said, "I'd rather ask someone I trusted better. I just read some of the coy letters you typed up for him about missing stock. I knew cows were worth about five times as much a head as sheep. I didn't know you had to produce a death certificate to prove you'd lost either. What good's a policy that pays off so infrequent?"

She sniffed and said she had no idea, adding, "Mr. Silas and no doubt the town law is going to be very vexed with you when I tell them you've been going through personal correspondence without so much as a knock on the door."

He tried, "I did knock."

But she shook her head and said, "Even if we somehow left the front door open there was simply no way you could have gotten into our business files without bending the laws on breaking and entering way out of shape."

She started to flounce out, to do whatever she thought the situation called for. Longram grabbed her and hauled her back against himself, soothing, "Let's not be all that hasty, Miss Poppy Jane. I have to allow you caught me breaking and entering, or entering, leastways, but do you really want to risk the ruin of your reputation for a man everyone calls a Shitzer?''

She let out a startled laugh and asked, ''Is that any way to talk to a lady?'' as she rubbed her well-padded pelvis against his in a manner that made him wonder who was shitting whom.

He caught himself grinding back against her as dirty, but said, ''Unless you're a lot more dumb and innocent than anyone has a right to be, working in a law office, you know your boss has been peddling almost worthless policies to stock outfits dumber than Kim Stover or L. J. Travis, and those are the outfits with the most to lose in these parts.''

She rubbed against him even bolder as she purred, ''What's that got to do with us? I told you to ask my boss, and if I don't get back there soon he's likely to come looking, if you follow my drift.''

He was commencing to. A roll in the feathers with such a sweet-moving and sort of dim butterball would be just what Dan Cupid prescribed for throbbing hard-ons, if she was that dim. It was a real pain in the ass to have a female suspect accuse you of rape when and if you had to arrest her.

He said, ''You go on back to Lawyer Spitzer with the papers he sent you for. Just don't tell him about anything going on between us, just yet.''

She pulled him closer with her plump arms and damned if she couldn't sort of clasp him with her love muscles, through both her duds and his own, as she purred, ''What's going on between us, and when, if not now?''

He resisted the desire to just hoist her damned skirt, haul out his throbbing erection, and shove it to her then and there, standing with her in the dark, as he declared, sincerely as he could manage, ''This is neither the time nor place, more's the pity, but I have a room at the hotel, if you'd like to meet me later.''

She protested that she'd just die if anyone in town ever even guessed she'd been up to a man's hotel room after dark. He soothed, "We'll shut the door. I mean after I sneak you up the back way, that is."

She told him he was just awful but that she wanted him awfully bad, now that they seemed to be conspiring against the rest of the world about something. When she asked just what it was he told her they'd have lots of time for pillow talk and sent her on her way with the papers her boss wanted, a pat on her fat rump she no doubt wanted, and a promise to wait in the dark doorway of a hat stop she knew of near the Beehive so they could pussyfoot upstairs for some of what they both wanted.

They agreed on eleven P.M. as the best time for their tryst and split up downstairs. He was too slick to follow her. He knew where she was going to begin with and figured there might be answers to other questions waiting for him at the Western Union.

There were.

The infernal Omaha Chamber of Commerce dispensed with one suspicion he'd had. They'd wired back that Universal Underwriters was indeed in the business of insuring stock or just about anything else and that they'd had no complaints about the outfit from anyone they might have swindled in recent memory. Allowing for local pride and the usual shit any insurance company put in the small print, Longram didn't see just cause to arrest anyone.

He sent off more messages of his own, including a progress report to Billy Vail, despite the poor progress he'd been making, and then, since ten P.M. had come and gone, he went back to his hotel to see just how clear the coast might be.

He saw it wasn't. The female night clerk he now knew as Marge beamed broadly across the lobby at him as he strode in. It would have been downright nasty not to go on over to her, so he did, and sure enough, she purred, "We've got a spanking-new bed in your room upstairs, and as you know I'm off at midnight. I made sure the handyman oiled the springs for us and tonight I'll know better than to leave the door unlocked behind me.''

He gulped and said, "That's, ah, mighty thoughtful of you, little darling, but would you get really sore if I asked for a rain check on your sweet surrender?"

She scowled in a manner warning of a temper she'd been smart enough to hide, so far, and allowed she'd be vexed as a wet hen stuffed with Spanish fly if he expected her to fend for herself after all the trouble she'd just gone to just to please him.

He soothed, "It ain't that my spirit ain't willing. It ain't that my flesh ain't weak. It's just that I might have to tangle with someone else tonight and I don't want to risk you getting hurt, hear?"

She sniffed and said, "I've a pretty good notion who you're out to tangle with. That pretty young Widow Stover was looking for you, here, not half an hour ago. She said she'd just missed you out to some sheep spread. So tell me true, is that who you've been two-timing me with, you brute?"

Longarm figured it was his turn to scowl. So he did, growling, "Hold on half a second, Marge. I fail to see how a man can two-time a gal he ain't said all that much mush to even one time."

She looked so hurt he felt obliged to add, "If I was out to wind up with another gal tonight, you have my word it wouldn't be Kim Stover."

Marge asked, "How come? Has she got the clap or something worse? Lord knows she's younger and prettier than me, damn her head to toe!"

He insisted, "Pretty is as pretty does, Marge. I don't want to tell tales about her for the same reasons you wouldn't want me telling tales about you. But you can take my word the Widow Stover and me were just never meant to be."

So Marge said, "Goody. Tonight I mean to teach you some French before I screw you silly!"

He saw there was no sense trying to reason with her. He

143

told her to hold the thought and that he'd be back when and if he got back. Then he went back outside, killed some time and wasted more thought in vain at the nearest saloon, and then it was pushing eleven and he had things figured about as good as he could get them to work.

He went to the hat shop Poppy Jane had mentioned and, finding it dark and deserted at that hour, moved into the door niche and lit a cheroot. As the fat gal had promised, he had a distant view of the front door of his hotel from here. After that his plans called for considerable changing. It seemed out of the question to try sneaking another gal into the Beehive past old Marge. But surely a hot buttered roll who knew her way around her own town so well would have suggestions on other parts of town to part her plump thighs. If not, he could likely satisfy her with a dark door way job and, if that didn't satisfy him, there'd still be good old Marge laying in wait to lay him right aboard that brand-new mattress.

He knew Billy Vail wouldn't approve of either notion. But he was done up here in the Red Desert, as far as the chore he'd been sent to do was concerned.

For if L. J. Travis had been dead all this time, it hardly mattered whether he'd cheated on his grazing fees or even bushwhacked the poor cuss from the BLM. Dead men told no tales. They weren't worth hanging and with Kim Stover's help little Belinda Travis would survive the modest costs of getting straight with the government again.

He still found all that crap about the Red Sash Gang annoying but hardly worth more of a serious lawman's time.

He'd have liked to know who'd sent at least three hired guns to do him in, and why, but he had to face the fact the answer lay down Denver way as well as it lay up this way. He'd gotten the cuss who'd pegged a shot at him and murdered poor Doris Drake down in Thayer Junction. The attempt of young Sandy MacPherson to pick a fight and win it had backfired, here in Honeycomb. He was pretty sure the one who'd murdered MacPherson after getting Lawyer

Spitzer to get him out of jail had to be the same silly son of a bitch in the lace boots who'd messed up his love life over yonder at the Beehive. Lawyer Spitzer likely knew the cuss on sight, at least, but the odds on anyone being in town after messing up that badly were slimmer than getting a tinhorn lawyer to tell a lawman the right time of day. So whoever was after said lawman was as likely to try again, with other pawns, until someone's luck ran out and one side or the other won.

Somewhere in the night a clock tolled eleven times and still no sign of Poppy Jane. He decided to finish one more cheroot before he packed it in. Marge, as he well knew, was a mighty fine lay he didn't have to play kid games with. Poppy Jane wasn't even as attractive, despite her soft, sweet-smelling bumps and grinds. The only thing she really had going for her was Longarm's cussed curiosity. Aside from being curious about how swell that grinding might feel, with no duds in the way, he still had some loose ends to tie up when it came to her slimy boss. If he treated her right she might just be willing to fill him in on their somewhat murky insurance and, of course, having a name to go with that lace-booted bastard who'd gotten a younger sidekick out of jail just to murder him might tip the scales of justice more the way Longarm liked to see 'em hanging.

He'd just finished the last smoke he'd allocated Poppy Jane and was fixing to pack it in for the night when he heard female footsteps coming along the wooden walk through the dismal street lighting of a late-night cow town. So he lit another cheroot as a subtle beacon of Eros, lest he shock some other lady prowling the dark streets on business of her own.

It worked, albeit not the way intended. As Kim Stover joined him in the dark doorway she gasped, "Custis! I've been searching high and low for you! Where have you been all this time? Have you been trying to avoid me, you big goof?"

He was already commencing to tingle below his gun rig,

knowing what always came next once he and old Kim met up in sunshine or in shadow. So he wasn't exactly lying when he replied, "Why would I want to do a dumb thing like that, honey lamb?"

To which she replied with a sad little sigh, "I didn't want to get my heart all mixed up again, either. But we have to get together and at least compare notes, darling. You know about Belinda and Ramon's problem. What are we going to do about the no-goods who butchered my poor Shorty Blare? Do you reckon it could have been that Red Sash Gang?"

He shook his head, saying, "That's about the one thing up this way I am at all sure of. There may or may not be a half-baked outlaw clan up Powder River way as favors such ridiculous means of holding up their jeans. Talk of them raiding down this way is either just talk or, at worse, a means to sell insurance on cows that shouldn't be let out to graze on such poor range to begin with."

She insisted, "Damn it, *somebody* shot poor Shorty, and if it wasn't the Red Sash Gang, who was it?"

He replied, "Somebody else, of course," as he morosely regarded a shadowy figure approaching them catty-corner across the street from the general direction of his hotel. That reminded him he couldn't take either Poppy Jane or the more sensibly built Kim Stover anywhere near the place, and he was about to ask Kim where she might be staying when he noticed the cuss coming their way wore laced boots and that the walking stick he seemed to be carrying looked more like a shotgun barrel as the range closed rapidly between them and it!

So he stiff-armed Kim with his left hand as he reached across his gut for his gun with his right. The sudden moves were not lost on the bastard in the laced boots. So the muzzle of his scattergun was rising as Kim landed on the plank walk with more than one splinter in her sweet rump, and Longarm's .44-40 came out of its holster spitting slugs.

It was still close. The mysterious booted figure jerked the

trigger of his ten gauge as he caught a round with his breast-bone and tried to stop another with his teeth, less neatly. So the full charge of buckshot blasted the plank walk Longarm was perched on to a big puff of toothpicks, albeit only one spent shot wound up imbedded harmlessly in one of Longarm's boot tips.

As he moved over toward Kim, keeping to the shadows of the overhang as he reached for some reload shells, the tough little widow gal produced a .32 from the garter holster she wore under her riding habit and propped herself up on one elbow to draw a bead on the man Longarm had just dropped. He warned her, "Don't. He's well done but he could have someone covering him from across the way. So leave us not break cover just yet."

He helped her back to her boot heels, though, and as doors and windows popped open all around and the street commenced to fill with curious humankind he told her she'd best put her bitty gun away while she could still do so in a modest fashion. He holstered his own reloaded revolver as Kim hoisted her skirts to tuck her smaller one away, between her creamy thighs.

When they saw Marshal Preston and a town deputy approaching the dead man from the far side Longarm thought it likely safe to call out to them and step into the light from the overhang of the hat shop. As they all met above the body sprawled by its shotgun in the dust, Preston asked if Longarm knew who'd gunned this poor cuss, or who said cuss might be.

Longarm said, "I cannot tell a lie. I did it with my little .44-40. I've no idea who he was. He was pointing that scattergun at me at the time."

Preston sighed and said it would all look a mite better on paper if Longarm could produce a witness to such an odd event. Kim Stover had drifted close enough to ask the town law, sweetly, if she might do.

Preston naturally knew the rich and powerful Widow Stover. He ticked his hat brim to her and soberly replied, gallantly, "With you backing his play a sheepherder could no doubt shoot the territorial governor and get off scot-free, Miss Kim."

His deputy cut in to observe, "Speaking of sheepherders, Dodge, ain't them walking boots the dead man's wearing, and didn't the night clerk at the Beehive recall lacy boots tearing across the lobby after that earlier attack on Longarm, here?"

Preston grinned down at the shot-up soul's ugly feet to exclaim, "By Jimmies, George, you may have hit the nail smack on the head! There can't be all that many strangers wandering about in sheepherder's boots with ten-gauge scatterguns in a town this size. So I'd say Longarm, here, just killed two birds with one stone!"

Longarm grimaced and said, "I put two rounds in him and only have one bird to show for it, so far."

Preston insisted, "He still adds up to the cuss who tried to blast you the other night, right after he got Sandy MacPherson out of jail. When he failed to silence you forever he settled for silencing young MacPherson and—"

"Back up," Longarm cut in. "To begin with, this mysterious cadaver never got anyone out of jail. It was Lawyer Spitzer with a writ of habeas corpus. I noticed the last time I was up in his office he keeps a drawer filled with 'em."

Preston nodded but said, "You're picking nits, pard. Spitzer the—Oops, ladies present, doesn't get folk out of jail from the love of his heart for humanity. I meant this dead cuss hired Lawyer Spitzer to get his pal out. Then they had to finish you off before MacPherson had to stand trial. A writ of habeas corpus just gets you out, it don't get you off forever unless the charges you was arrested on fail to pan out."

Longarm shushed him to say, "You're lecturing a lawman on basic law, Dodge. Meanwhile, the lawyer with all the answers could be on his way to Canada. Would you like to tag along and listen while I see if he's finished packing yet?"

Dodge Preston said he certainly would. His deputy, Kim Stover and at least a dozen townsmen seemed to want to tag along as well. But as Longarm led the foot parade to the west from Main Street Preston said, ''I don't see how you're going to get much out of Lawyer Spitzer if he means to just hang tough and cite attorney-client privileges.''

Kim Stover, who knew more about legal matters than your average cowgirl, opined the town marshal had a point. So Longarm growled, ''I don't give a bucket of warm spit about that tinhorn's professional privileges. He can tell me privately and off the record if he wants, but tell me he will, if I have to wring his slimy neck!''

Chapter 12

Somebody else had already done so, though, by the time
Longarm and his party arrived at the slippery lawyer's frame
bungalow near the dead end of a dark, dirty street. It was
Preston's deputy, George, who actually found Lawyer
Spitzer's body inside when he slipped around to the back
door to see if he could find out why nobody answered
Longarm's imperious pounding on the front door.

As they all filed in and Preston turned the wick of an oil
lamp brighter to shed more light on the subject, the first
thing anyone noticed was the red silk scarf, or sash, knotted
around the fat throat of the fat corpse on the kitchen floor.
Longarm had no call to argue with the townsfolk saying
that was Spitzer the Shitzer. But he'd pictured the wily
lawyer as a lean and hungry small-town Scrooge. On re-
flection it figured such a greedy cuss might run to lard.
Dodge Preston hunkered down to run his hands over the
already sort of disgusting cadaver as Kim, being a female
as curious as most of her kind, commenced to poke about

near the stove, noting the cast iron was still warm and that there were still a few embers glowing in the firebox.

The town marshal volunteered, "Robbery couldn't have been the killer's reason, Longarm. This old boy still has over five dollars on him."

Longarm growled, "I wasn't suggesting you arrest him for vagrancy. Are you sure he was strangled, though?"

Preston shot a puzzled glance up at Longarm to reply, "See for yourself. This sash is knotted tight as she'll go, pard."

Longarm glanced at Kim Stover's trim back, then shot Preston a warning look as he muttered, "Smell for yourself and then tell me you're sure an old boy with a gut that gigantic died of strangulation."

Preston's jaw dropped. Then he nodded. He knew better than to repeat what Longarm already knew. They both knew any critter being choked to death convulses and shits its bowels empty before it gives up the ghost entire.

Preston muttered, "We'd best have the doc make sure. A corpse this size could absorb a heap of bullet holes or stab wounds and still seem about as neat, at first glance."

Kim turned from the stove to state, "He was killed during or not long after entertaining company. Two people he knew well enough to give coffee and cake."

Longarm knew better than to ask her how she knew. Old George did, so she sniffed and said, "Three cups, three saucers, three cake plates and the silverware to go with 'em in the dry sink. The coffeepot's half filled and the breadbox half empty. Add it up."

George did and said, "I swann."

Longarm said, "Let's try her this way: It's just plain redundant to call a lawyer a crooked lawyer, but Spitzer was smart as well as true to his craft. So they fibbed to him when they had him spring Sandy MacPherson from jail for 'em. He wouldn't have risked his own neck had he known MacPherson was a hired gun really out for blood."

Preston nodded knowingly and said, "Seeing Mac-

Pherson laid out dead and disfigured after you'd found his body out in the sage must have been an educational experience for old Spitzer here.''

Longarm nodded and said, ''Earlier this evening he sent his plump Poppy Jane back to his office for some papers. She caught me up in their office. I asked her not to tell her boss but he was her boss, and you know what they say about telegraph, telephone, and tell a woman.''

Kim Stover muttered, ''Gee, thanks.''

Longarm just shot her a sheepish grin and continued, ''When Spitzer found out I was asking all sorts of questions about him he knew he had two choices. He could just pack up and run for it before I closed in, or he could get his lace-booted client, associate, or whatever to do the same. Right here in this very kitchen he told one or more crooks he meant to give them a modest lead and then bare all to me and Uncle Sam, with results you can see for yourselves on the floor.''

Everyone murmured a mite. Then Kim said, ''I know poor Poppy Jane. We have to find her before those Red Sash killers do! Can't any of you see that if her boss knew who they were, Poppy Jane would know who they were and—''

''You could be right, or you could be wrong,'' Longarm cut in, nodding at the dirty dishes in the sink to her right. ''If Spitzer was entertaining two men, one of 'em, at least, could still be running loose out yonder in the dark. If Poppy Jane had coffee and cake with her boss and old lace boots, she has nobody but me to worry about. Since she ain't on the floor with her boss right now, it's safe to assume she left before anyone here saw fit to harm her.''

Kim said, ''I know where she lives. It's not far from the town house I keep here in Honeycomb. But what danger do you, of all people, present to the poor little butterball, Custis?''

Longarm smiled thinly and said, ''It depends a lot on how many fibs she's told me so far. I know I got her in at

153

least a couple she'll no doubt try to call white lies. But why don't we just go ask her?''

He turned back to Dodge Preston to ask, "Do you reckon you know how to tidy this part up, Marshal?''

Preston nodded and said, "You'll find both bodies over at the doc's when you get done with Miss Poppy Jane. We get a copy of her deposition if it's worth filing, right?''

Longarm nodded and nudged Kim Stover, murmuring, "Let's go. I'm sort of glad you keep your own place for when you're in town on visit. Is it nice as that cabin you used to own up to the Wind River range?''

She confided, "I still own it. But you'll find the dear little bungalow here in Honeycomb a lot handier, honey.''

They headed for Poppy Jane's cottage first, to save having to get dressed again when they went calling on her. For Longarm had known as sure as the lovely blonde had called him honey in public that he was just plain doomed to delve her depths once more with his suddenly shameless shaft.

He knew she'd abandoned all hope of acting sensible about the way things had to be, as well. But since it would have been sort of crude to throw her down in the dust and get right to it, he contented himself for the moment with asking about Kim's visit to the law office just before his first one. Kim said Poppy Jane had been mistaken about her being there to talk to Spitzer about stock insurance. As they strode on down the dark street she explained, "I have my property and hired help covered by a group policy from the Cattlemen's Protective Association. They don't insure stock, exactly. They have sort of sinister gents out scouting for range wolves, range thieves and so on.''

"You still went to see Spitzer about something," he insisted.

She hesitated, then said, "I suppose I can tell you. No federal statutes are involved. I wouldn't hire such a tinhorn to draw up a bill of sale for me, personal, but he is, or was, a well-known fixer. I wanted his views on a delicate marital matter.''

Longarm asked who she was planning to marry up with, this time, and she said with a sigh, ''Not me, silly. I told you that time in Chicago that I seem to have a fatal effect on husbands. My little chum, Belinda Travis, would surely like to marry up with her good-looking ramrod, Ramon Eskabal, only. . . . Never mind, I told her I'd ask nobody but a lawyer sworn to secrecy, dear.''

Longarm nodded and said, ''Belinda ain't all that swell at keeping family secrets. I don't think Wyoming Territory is likely to raise a fuss over a purely white Basque boy getting hitched to a lady of some color. They might if things were the other way around and a colored cuss was likely to wind up in charge of all that land and livestock. What did the late Lawyer Spitzer have to say about it?''

''Nothing. I never got to talk to him about the sweet kids. Are you saying they should just go ahead and get hitched without saying anything about anyone's family tree, Custis?''

He nodded and replied, ''Why not? Did you swear you was blonde all over the times you got hitched, honey?''

She said she followed his drift but didn't want to dwell on the dead past. He asked how far they had to go, and when she told him the fat gal lived in that bitty place standing ghostly on the corner with no lights lit inside he said, ''Bueno. We'd best leave you on this side of the street while I work around to the back. Barging up to the front door of a blacked-out house can take as much as fifty years off a lawman's life. So I try to avoid dumb moves like that whenever possible.''

Without waiting to see what Kim might have to say about that, he left her by a moonlit picket fence on one side and crossed over to the other, drawing his .44-40 along the way. He forked his long legs over yet another fence and worked his way between two houses, paying no attention as a small ferocious dog yapped somewhere inside one house

155

or the other. By the time an elderly cuss came to a back door to call out, "I see you, sonny, and I got me a gun, here!" Longarm was over his back fence into the alley. So he felt no call to answer, and just eased on up to open a back gate near some ashcans and eased on across Miss Poppy Jane's back garth, checking out the outhouse to make sure his back was safe as he took his time picking the lock of her back door.

It wasn't too tough. The house smelled mighty perfumed inside. As he worked his way through the apparently empty cottage he almost shot Kim Stover when they met in the front hall. He hissed, "Don't! It's me, and it's lucky for you that you're wearing a different perfume! How'd you get in and is that a gun you're pointing at me, doll face?"

The pretty young widow woman lowered her .32 to her side as she explained, "The front door was open. I didn't think I had to worry about Poppy Jane mistaking me for a burglar, Custis."

He swore under his breath and said, "That wasn't what I was worried about. There's no sign of Spitzer's secretary on the premises. There's no sign she packed up, earlier, to go anywhere. I can't speak for any burglars, but there's all sorts of gewgaws spread about the house that I can't see her just leaving town without. One gets the impression from both her figure and furniture that old Poppy Jane places a heap of value on her creature comforts."

Kim sniffed and said, "Some of that sandalwood scent smells nice and fresh. I'll bet she went out to meet some sneaky swain by the light of the silvery moon!"

Longarm started to say something neither of them might have ever forgiven him for saying. He decided, instead, "There's no law saying a single gal can't meet anyone she fancies, anywhere she might have told him to meet her. I'd still best peer into the crawl space under this house, though."

Kim followed him outside, asking, "Are you serious? I thought we agreed over at the lawyer's place that nobody had any call to hurt poor Poppy Jane. I never told her my business with her boss. Wouldn't it have been awfully dumb for a real crook if he, she, or it let such a silly in on any serious secrets?''

Longarm finished prying some lattice skirting out of his way and struck a match to peer about under the crawl space as he grunted, ''Nobody here but us spiders. I hope you're right about the fat gal being dumb and innocent. She was helping Spitzer sell overpriced stock insurance on shaky grounds, and if she was only a dupe, where could she be right now?''

Kim repeated her suggestion that the dumpy thing was just out after some loving. He didn't think he'd better say Poppy Jane could doubtless screw pretty good standing up with all her duds on. But the memory inspired him to shove the lattice back in place and rise to full height, both ways, saying, ''Wherever she's gone, she ain't here, and didn't you say your own place is only a short walk?''

She laughed and said, ''I see great minds still run in the same channels. We can save some steps cutting down the back alley.''

So they did, entering the better-kept but no larger back garth of Kim's town house via her alley gate. Despite its neat trim the place was in fact but a bitty frame bungalow, meant only for a place Kim could hang her hat when she got down this way. He was just as glad they weren't at her fancy cabin up at her more Alpine home spread. Her servants knew better than to even notice when the boss lady had an overnight guest. But it always seemed to Longarm that someone had to be listening, and likely grinning, when old Kim got on top to really test the bedsprings.

Crossing toward the smaller back door of the more modest town house, Longarm was mildly surprised to spy yet another outhouse. Indoor plumbing had been possible, if not entirely practical, ever since that inventive Englishman, Mr. Crapper, had devised a neater way to shit. The running water, pipes, and such were still a mite unhandy in places

157

still as countrified as Honeycomb. So he saw no need to comment on the sanitary arrangements of a place that was, after all, only a glorified camp site for his rich young hostess.

But he felt it would be even more awkward to use an outhouse later, barefooted as well as bare assed, so as she unlocked her back door he murmured, "You go on in and I'll be along directly."

Being a Victorian, Kim didn't ask why. Gentle folk of their era managed to waft through a world of outdoor plumbing and ankle-deep horseshit in the streets without appearing to notice.

Since this took a certain amount of nonchalance learned young, Kim simply said she'd start without him if he didn't hurry, and went on in to get set for bed as Longarm turned to heed the call of nature before it called loud enough to distract his old organ grinder from its true mission in life.

So Poppy Jane had the drop on him when he opened the door of Kim's outhouse to discover her there with a big .45 aimed right at his heart, point-blank. The fat gal hissed, "If you let out one peep you're dead!"

He nodded soberly and weighed the chances of his getting to his own gun, cross-draw, with her .45's muzzle smack against the front of his shirt. He didn't know whether he could gun a woman, anyway, so he gently asked her, "How come our hitherto friendly relationship seems to be turning out so unfriendly, Miss Poppy Jane? I was waiting on the pleasure of your company, where you said I ought to wait, when that shotgun-toting cuss in the lace boots came to keep your tryst with me. You told your boss you'd caught me going through his drawers, and you were just teasing me when you implied I might go through your drawers, huh?"

She laughed, lewdly, and said, "That's close enough. If it's any comfort I was mighty tempted when we got sort of close as we both threw bull at one another."

He sighed and said, "We'd best stop doing that, then. If you knew enough to lay for me here you likely know as much or more than I can tell, right?"

She nodded and said, "I could have back-shot both of you as you crossed the yard with that blonde bitch. I've got to get out of town. I dasn't go back to my place, even for eating money. So I'll give you three guesses why you're still alive, and I may even let you live if you play your cards right with me."

He nodded soberly and said, "You want getaway money and a pony to get away on. I got a little over sixty dollars on me and, of my two ponies at the livery, I'd say the buckskin will carry you farther and faster, so shall we ease on over?"

She shoved the gun muzzle against him harder, saying, "First we get rid of your side arm. Then we take a little walk. You can unbuckle with just one hand. So do it, with your left one, and consider that this old Colt in my own dainty hand is hair triggered as well as full cocked."

Just thinking about that was enough to make a man wet his jeans, not even having to go. But he managed not to, somehow, as he gingerly unbuckled his gun rig and reluctantly let it fall to the gravel about his boots. As he did so she deftly removed his pocket watch and derringer with her free hand. He muttered, "That was mighty cold of you, Miss Poppy Jane."

She favored him with a throaty chuckle and said, "Look on the bright side. Now that I have you completely in my power I may just let you snack on me. Have you ever gone down on a gal with a gun to your head, handsome?"

He had to chuckle at the dumb picture, and seeing she seemed so amused at the notion as well, he asked, "When might you want us to pose so bawdy, ma'am?"

"Not in town, you sly sweet-talker. I might take you out on the desert with me a ways, since we have two ponies and plenty of moonlight to work with."

He started to ask if that was how young Sandy Mac-Pherson had wound up so far from town before they'd finished him off. He didn't think he even wanted to ask whether the kid had gotten any before she or her lover in the lace boots had turned him into wolf grub. She told him to turn around and head for the back gate, nice and easy. As he stepped clear of his own gun she told him to hold it, and she hunkered down to gather his rig up, saying, "I can use this, if I punch extra holes in the strap. I wish I had a split skirt like that snippy Miss Kim rides about in. You don't have a side saddle for me at the livery, do you?"

He said there could be one in the tack room, for all he knew, and added, "Let's get cracking, if you mean to get your sweet self over the horizon by sunrise."

As he headed for the back gate she followed, close, with her gun muzzle smack against his spine, saying, "You don't fool me. You want to get us both clear of Miss Kim before she comes looking for you out here and I get to shoot her, right?"

He didn't answer. He couldn't think of anything to say to a lady of such obviously murderous intent. As they approached the gate she warned, "Don't get cute as you step into the alley. I got you in my clutches cold and there's nothing that can save you, now!"

Then Kim Stover proved her wrong. Longarm dove headfirst into a clump of backyard lilac as the first .32 round spangled into the bigger gun Poppy Jane was holding. So he only found out, later, that Kim had blown it out of the fat gal's hand before putting four more rounds in her plumper parts, snarling, "Ruin my evening, will you?" in a most unladylike manner, while the fat gal wailed, "Don't kill me! I'll be a good little girl from now on if only you'll make it stop hurting me so!"

Longarm sat up amid ruined lilac stems, calling out, "You heard her, Kim! Don't finish her off before we've heard all the dear little gal has to say!"

But as he crawled on his hands and knees over to the considerable remains, he saw Poppy Jane had sort of wilted away on them, and as Kim came closer, reloading, he said so, adding, "I wish you'd been content to just blast her off her feet, honey. Thanks to that final round in her fat head we're going to have to figure out the finer details for ourselves."

Then he got to his feet, stepped into the outhouse, and took a good long leak while he still had the chance. Gunfire sure attracted a heap of attention in a town as dull as Honeycomb tended to be, most nights.

Chapter 13

If gunning the mysteriously murderous Poppy Jane in her own backyard didn't completely ruin Kim's plans for the evening, it certainly put a crimp in her determination to tickle Longarm's fancy with her fancier parts. It was way after midnight before all concerned agreed to let the bodies and other matters rest for now so everyone could catch at least a few winks of sleep.

Longarm was pretty sure everyone else in town had been asleep some time before he just had to haul it out of Kim a spell and give them both a chance to catch their second wind. As they lay there in the sweet, chilly pre-dawn darkness, sharing goosebumps and a smoke, Kim snuggled her naked body even closer to his and murmured, "That was lovely, darling. Do you reckon we'll get to do it again?"

He let her puff on his cheroot as she played with his belly hairs, assuring her, "Just let me get my pulse down and my pecker back up to normal and you'll be sorry you asked such a foolish question, you pretty little thing."

She lost his cheroot somewhere on her side of the bed as she rolled halfway aboard him, saying, "I wasn't talking about right now, you big silly. I know you told Marshal Preston and the deputy coroner you'd get back together with them this afternoon, after you've had time to verify some more suspicions by telegraphing hither and yon. I was asking if we'd be able to fornicate so fine once you'd finished tying up the loose ends of your mission here in Wyoming Territory."

He yawned, patted her bare behind with one hand and stretched the other arm as far as he could, soothing, "It's likely to take me the coming weekend and more to get a handle on all that's happened since Billy Vail sent me off so simple. I got about two-thirds of the basic facts figured out, while the rest elude me entire. So why don't we just sort of sleep on 'em?"

She protested she wasn't the least bit sleepy, adding, "I tried to follow you as you were explaining things to Dodge Preston and the others, Custis. But you used such technical terms, and I'd never heard of some of the people you seemed to think had something to do with that monstrous fat girl and . . . By the way, might she have had the least right to assume you'd want to go down on her?"

He soothed, "Hell, I never even had a finger in her." Which was true, when one considered exactly how he and Poppy Jane had felt one another up.

Kim felt him up, more intimately, and said, "Goody. If you're going to have to linger up this way a spell for Marshal Vail, what say we go on up to my mountain cabin this weekend so you can sort of ponder the mystery undisturbed, darling?"

It was tempting. He knew just how sweetly Kim could disturb a man. He knew how disturbed she acted when a man announced it was time for him to ride on, too. So he got a comfortable grip on her cute little tailbone and told her, "We'd best stick tighter to the scenes of the crimes. The crimes we know most about, at any rate. If you don't want to snuggled down for some shut-eye, suppose you go over the help you were giving Belinda and Ramon some more. You're right about it being tough to concentrate with fat gals oozing blood and everyone trying to talk at once.''

She grimaced, kissed his collarbone, and said, ''Nobody on or about the Travis spread did anything wrong, Custis. My second husband and me did lots of business with old L. J. Travis when he was alive and I'd grown fond of little Belinda. So when she came to me with the news her father had died natural but intestate on her and that she and Ramon had buried him in unseemly and informal haste—''

''I understand how an only child with disadvantages as to race and gender could have felt reluctant to throw herself on the mercy of a probate court run by the enemy,'' he cut in. ''What I find more mysterious is the dumb jam old L. J. Travis left his daughter in, if you say he was such a decent old sheepherder. I saw no signs of overstocking anywhere near the Travis home spread. So why do you reckon he abused open range the way the BLM accused him?''

Kim forked her smooth thigh farther across his hips and began to see if she could get it up for the both of them as she replied, only half interested, ''I think that can be explained as a sloppy stock tally complicated by a dumb attempt at charity on my part.'' Then she tried to get it in her, half hard, only to hear Longarm protest, ''Don't change the subject now, for Pete's sake! How could the gents collecting grazing fees for the BLM confuse anything you did with anything your dusky sheepherding chums might have done?''

She persisted in her determined efforts to impale herself on a shaft a mite too big for her opening when it was hard, explaining, ''Old L.J. must have been sicker than he let on for quite a spell, before he just fell dead entire. I didn't know this, of course. I'd have fetched him a doctor had I known he needed one. When Belinda told me there were bills to pay and that her dad didn't seem to be paying her

165

much mind I tried to help them out without hurting an old and not-quite-white man's pride.''

Longarm's pride and joy was beginning to rise to the occasion by now. He pleaded with her to finish while there was still time to think of anything but her warm innards. She said, ''Putting it simply, I arranged to have some of my own mutton sold on the market as produce of the Travis herd. I didn't think L.J. or even Belinda and Ramon would see through my well-meant little prank.''

Then it was in her. But Longarm still managed to laugh and say, ''In sum I was sent on a fool's mission. There never was any overstocking on the part of anyone.''

She didn't answer. She was too busy bouncing. He lost a lot of interest in raising sheep or cattle, now that she had him raised so swell. But the one and only thing Longarm found the least bit wrong about fucking was that sooner or later you had to finish, if there was to be any point to it at all.

So after they'd finished, with him on top and their heads somehow down at the foot of her bed, he was able to say as he let it go on soaking in her, ''That still leaves the missing process server from the BLM. But I'll take your word the Travis clan being decent as any other sheep-herders, and Billy Vail will likely buy him just getting lost up this way in the tricky distances and disgusting climate. The writ both of us were asked to serve on old L.J. only demanded he or his lawyer appear in court to show cause why the government shouldn't prosecute him as a range hog.''

Kim protested, ''But, dear, he's dead and never abused his grazing fees to begin with!''

He moved in her experimentally, sensed they both needed a mite more time to tinge some more, and replied, ''I just said that. I told you my boss sent me up here on a fool's errand. It wasn't the first time crooks on the scene doing something else assumed I was on to their skulduggery. A guilty conscience can lead one into deeper trouble than the original temptation.''

She moved her trim hips teasingly and purred, ''Do you aim to satisfy my curiosity about that wicked fat gal and her sneaky boss or do you aim to really satisfy me, lover man?''

He chuckled fondly, kissed her soft throat, and said, ''Both. We'd best work on curiosity, first. Sooner or later I got to put on my infernal pants and wire Billy Vail what happened. He's likely to be sore enough about the land office wasting our time. I'd better have my facts on the stock insurance flimflam straight in my head.''

She asked him in that case to take it out while he told her. So he did. But he resisted the impulse to grope for another smoke, knowing they cost him three for a nickle, and knowing how tough it was to finish one in bed with such sweeter temptations. As they cuddled into a more conversational pose he explained, ''Universal Underwriters is a distant but fairly honest firm. Keep the part about distance in mind. They do sell stock insurance, albeit at impractical prices for sheep or even cows. No insurance company can afford to accept small premiums and pay handsomely for any property as likely to get lost as livestock.''

She murmured, ''I know. That's why I don't carry insurance on any of my own stock. But wasn't Lawyer Spitzer selling an awful lot of it?''

He held her tighter, saying, ''He was and he wasn't. He and his help spread rumors about a mythical gang to get everyone edgy about their stock. We're still working on whether they ever got around to running any uninsured stock into a swamp or over a rimrock. Tales of red-sashed ruffians and the natural losses as go with grazing such marginal range might have been enough.''

Kim repressed a yawn and rubbed some blonde thatch against his naked hip to keep them both wide awake as she asked, ''Where was the federal felony, then? I mean, sure, it's mean to tell fibs just to sell something, but how often does Billy Vail send you out after snake oil salesmen, Custis?''

He chuckled and said, "Keep it in mind he never sent me after Spitzer to begin with. He pushed sharp business practices way past simple lying about the product, albeit you're right about him failing to bust any federal statutes. Like I said, a guilty conscience can drive some crooks over the edge.''

"Are you going to tell me what all the excitement was about?'' she demanded. "I saw you and Dodge Preston going over those insurance policy blanks you found in Spitzer's bungalow. I looked at one myself. I fail to see how any company could make a profit at such generous terms, but you say the company he was repping for out here on the Red Desert was legitimate, and if that's so I don't mind telling you I'd have bought such a policy myself.''

Longarm chuckled and said, "That's how come they were selling so many, and collecting a thirty-percent commission on each and every one. As you no doubt noticed, the first page of the four-page policy said that stock run off by thieves would be paid for at current market prices, as posted on the eastern exchange.''

She nodded and said, "Like I said, mighty generous. I've never heard of anyone insuring anything for its possible top dollar.''

"Of course you haven't. Why repair or even repaint an insured house when all you'd have to do to get a new one just as fine would be to burn the old one down? Would anyone with a lick of sense go to the trouble of rearing a calf to market size, and shipping the same all the way to market, when one could just report it stolen and cash the resulting check?''

She said, "Well, there was that small-print rider on page four that only offered a couple of dollars a head for losses due to agues and accidents, and I can see how tough it might be to prove a cow was stolen instead of just strayed, but—''

"That part was the way the policy really read," Longarm cut in. "They had to leave that one clause because it was printed, however fine, on the page the client had to *sign*, see?"

She gasped and said, "I'm starting to! Are you saying Spitzer had switched the *other pages* of that overly generous policy, just so he could sell insurance easy?"

Longarm shrugged his bare shoulders and assured her, "Only the first page, as Preston and me figure it. All the generous words are up front, where a semi-literate stockman would look first. The other pages, as you noticed, read sort of long-winded and stuffy. Once Spitzer had a sucker signed up he just had to switch that first page or just lose it, since the so-called second page works well enough as the first page of a standard contract drawn up by a fuss-and-feathers law clerk."

She marveled, "He and that wicked fat girl only had to send the regular policy on to the company, along with the client's check or money order, and then they'd get back that handsome commission with nobody the wiser!"

Then she proved she was really smart by adding, "Hold on, dear. That nasty little Sandy MacPherson did mention the Red Sash Gang, as did those two real outlaws down at the Smithfield spread, and have you forgotten the red sash around Spitzer's own fat neck?"

He grunted in disgust and muttered, "All of that's bush-league easy. Beginning backward, Poppy Jane or old Lacey Boots left that length of red silk around his neck after killing him less dramatical. The deputy coroner is still working on that. I just said the whole bunch was spreading bull about the Red Sash Gang as a means to sell insurance. Sandy MacPherson and Lacey Boots were on Spitzer's payroll. Bowie Bascom and Concho Landers were just mean saddle tramps who'd heard rumors of a big gang out this way and were looking to join up with 'em, if ever they discovered how. Meanwhile they'd stumbled on a helpless nester family to prey on and, lucky for the same, I stumbled on them.

After I took out those lowlifes I came on to Honeycomb, not even knowing Spitzer and his bunch by name and—''

"They jumped to hasty conclusions about you!'' she cut in with an incredulous laugh, grabbing him where it almost hurt. "Lucky for me, Spitzer knew, as a member of the local courthouse gang, that there just wasn't anything else going on that any serious lawman might be interested in. Once they added two and two to come up with seven or eight, it all falls neatly in place.''

He wasn't quite ready to put it back in place. So he said, "Billy Vail is still going to want to know how I managed to get your sheepherder, Shorty, killed on us. I confess I've just no idea what to tell him or anyone else about that!''

She sighed and said, "Thank heavens he left no friends or relations I have to write to about that. Couldn't he have just been done in by some wandering two-legged animal with a mean disposition and some bullets he didn't know what else to do with, dear?''

Longarm grimaced at the window curtains, noticing how light a shade of gray the sky was getting now, as he growled, "Sloppy, even though that's the way we wind up writing off a heap of loose ends for lack of anything neater. I can't help feeling I sort of sent trouble Shorty's way when I winged that tall gray rascal down in Thayer Junction.''

She soothed, "There's no call for you to feel guilty, then. You left our Shorty alive and well amid the Tanglewaters after finding that other cuss dead in the company of that stolen thoroughbred. You left said thoroughbred miles away with that nester gal. So Shorty Blare must have been killed for his own pony later, long after you'd ridden on, right?''

He kissed the part of her blonde hair before he said, "That's the way it reads. I'd feel a heap better if I had more names and sensible reasons to go with everybody I've met up with since I started out from Denver.''

She suggested Lawyer Spitzer could have been behind the trouble down in Thayer Junction. He shook his sincerely puzzled head and said, "Lawyer Spitzer was a small-town

170

crook at best. Poppy Jane seems to have been the more deadly of the species, and you didn't know I was coming, did you?''

She purred that he could come all he liked in her. He warned her she'd rue that last remark if ever he could get it up again, and continued, ''The gent who tried to back-shoot me way down by the U.P. line won't work for beans as a hired gun working for Spitzer and his fat female accomplice.''

She asked how else the cuss worked. He screwed her some more instead of explaining about poor Doris Drake. It only would have served to piss Kim off, and that tall silvery haired cuss he'd finally tracked down wouldn't work as her nasty baby brother or one of his snotty young side-kicks. He forgot about the dead Doris as Kim got mighty lively in his arms. It was her, later, who dredged up the dead men down in the Tanglewaters. She said, ''Ramon Eskabal tells me they found what looked to be turned over dirt along the edge of a reedy slough. That would have been where you planted the one you nailed, right?''

He grimaced and said, ''To tell the truth I left him for the crows. I didn't think Shorty would mind. It was over a mile downwind of his camp. I reckon Shorty must have thought it best to bury him after all, I'm ashamed to say. Why are we having this grim conversation, Kim?''

She replied, ''I thought it best to get it straight that your back-shooter was really and truly dead when you rode on. What if some of his pals came looking for him, figured it had been Shorty, not you, as shot their pal and— Hold on, Ramon never said anything about him being dug up. You must think I'm pretty silly.''

He frowned thoughtfully up at the ceiling as he soberly replied, ''No sillier than me. Why would a lone sheepherder want to lead strangers to a grave site out in a swamp to begin with?''

She agreed that sounded dumb and said, ''I see what you mean about just having to write some things off as mysterious. I reckon we'll just never know for certain what happened to poor old Shorty.''

That almost got past him. He was in the middle of a yawn as she said it. He said, "Shorty Blare never struck me as all that old, or all that short, come to study on it.''

She reached down to pull the sheet up over them as she yawned, and said, "It would have been mean to call a really short gent Shorty. Shorty Blare didn't mind, because he was around six foot four or more, see?''

His eyes popped wide open as he flatly stated, "I saw no such thing down younder. The young sheepherder who asked me to call him Shorty wasn't quite six feet tall, and you say the real Shorty Blare was old?''

She snuggled closer under the sheet with him to reply, "Not *old* old, Dear. I suspect he was pushing fifty, with his hair going gray sort of premature. Why do you refer to him as the *real* Shorty Blare, Custis? Have you met any other Shorty Blare's in recent memory?''

He started to sit up. He decided it made more sense to get some damned sleep before he strapped on his gun rig some more, and there was just no way he could leave town before he and Kim satisfied a coroner's jury they'd been right to gun down Lacey Boots and Miss Poppy Jane the night before.

So he lay back down beside the beautiful blonde to explain, "The younger gent I found in the company of Shorty Blare's sheep and such wasn't Shorty Blare. He was a big fibber. After I left he just lit out, alive and well, aboard the real sheepherder's pony, see?''

It was her turn to stare wide awake as she protested, "Then how come Ramon and the Travis herders found Shorty Blare down younder so dead, if he was never there to begin with?''

Longarm enfolded her in his arms, soothing, "It's a long tedious tale, and anyone can see how tired you are, little darling. Just take my word I got it all worked out, now, and let's see if we can catch us forty winks.''

She said she'd try, on condition he tickle her fancy just one more time. So he did, and never had to tell her the ways he'd made poor Doris Drake climax before she'd been killed by a really no-good sneaky son of a bitch.

Chapter 14

Billy Vail and deputies Dutch and Smiley were waiting at the Union Depot the afternoon Longarm got back to Denver aboard the Burlington Day Coach from Cheyenne.

Longarm had felt no call to change back into his tobacco tweed office duds, just yet. So as he came along the platform packing his saddle and possibles on one hip Vail greeted him with, "Jesus H. Christ, you look like a trail herder and smell like a whorehouse. What's all this shit about murderous sheepherders running loose in downtown Denver, damn it?"

Longarm sighed and said, "I sure wish you weren't so cheap about us charging messages by telegraph to the taxpayers, boss. Trying to save a nickel a word makes for some confusion, I suspect."

He turned to Deputy Smiley, a morose-looking breed who'd never smiled in human memory, to ask, "Might you have checked out that boardinghouse I wired in about, old son?"

Smiley nodded soberly and said, "The kid brother of that girl who died in Thayer Junction is still living there. He just got a job in the stockyards, punching beef aboard the railroad cars with a patent prod."

His more cheerful looking but if anything meaner sidekick, Dutch, said, "Finding him and where he was working was easy. How come you didn't want him picked up if you gave shit-one about where he might be found these days?"

Longarm explained, "I was out to save myself a needless albeit possible side trip to Durango. As the self-proclaimed Kid Chinks, our Elroy Drake got his fool self too famous for comfort, up Durango way, by chasing me out of the Chapman Saloon one night last April."

Smiley stared sternly at Longarm to demand, "You let such a piss ant start up with you and live? I got to be missing something here."

Dutch soothed, "I got it figured, Smiley. Old Custis, here, has more delicate manners than you and me. He took pity on the young shit, figuring him for drunk and harmless, only to discover, later, that the boy was bragging on backing down his betters!"

Billy Vail cocked a bushy brow at Longarm to demand, "Is that what this is all about, you perfumed saddle tramp? You called us down here from the Federal Building to back your play as you blow away some two-bit pest?"

Longarm shook his head and said, "Just the opposite, Billy. As I wired you from Honeycomb, I had to leave a few details unresolved, including the cologne you keep chiding me about. For when a man has the chance to go, he'd better, and bathing facilities are limited on the Red Desert."

Vail growled, "Never mind why you stink so pretty. How come you asked for so much backup just to take one bushleague bandito alive?"

Longarm soothed, "I never asked for you, personal, boss. I asked for at least two backup men because that boardinghouse has a side cellar door as well as a back way out if it's built at all like the other ones along Wazee Street. As to his being a bandito, even bush league, you could be inflating his rep even more than he's ever bragged. I just want to see him and tell him about his sister being dead, for openers. We'll see what happens next.''

Dutch nodded sagely and said, ''I reckon I follow your drift. His big sister came to you to begin with to see if she could make peace between the ferocious Longarm and notorious Kid Chinks, so—''

''Aw, stuff a sock in it and let's get it over with,'' Longarm cut in. So nobody argued further about it as he led the parade to the check room, checked his saddle and possibles, including the Winchester, and said, ''It might save us a trudge up to Wazee Street if we explore the stockyards, first. They're closer and he ought to still be on duty there if he's even halfway honest about earning his own keep.''

Kid Chinks was, working as Elroy Drake according to the straw boss they first consulted on the far side of the depot. The straw boss offered to save Longarm and his pals some walking by sending a Mex kid to fetch their new cowpoke. But Longarm said they sort of wanted to surprise old Elroy, albeit he warned Billy Vail there was no call to risk cowshit on *his* fresh-polished boots.

Vail allowed he wouldn't miss whatever Longarm had in mind for the world. But as they all trudged across the dusty tracks and railroad ballast spotted with fresh cow pats, Vail asked just what his senior deputy had in mind. So Longarm sighed and admitted, ''I'm not dead certain. If this interview with the dead gal's brother goes the way I hope it may, we'll have that last case wrapped snug as a bug in a rug. If it don't I'll sure wind up feeling dumber than usual.''

Vail admitted, ''Long-winded as your night letter might have been, you lost me as regards some leftovers. Who was Lacey Boots and what ever happened to that Indian cowhand and bearded white sheepherder?''

The Denver railroad yards ran north and south between the South Platte River and the downtown business district. So the freight train stopped on the siding ahead of them had its ass end aimed at them as they approached. Longarm said, "Swing to the left. The loading chutes the straw boss mentioned would be up the tracks on the shady side. I didn't think it worth a nickel a word to inform you old Two Lodges was known to some of the boys in Honeycomb as an honest Injun, or that Spitzer's secretary's paramour and errand boy was an otherwise worthless Basque called Tomas Heguy. All that shit was simply a shady insurance scheme that snowballed all out of proportion 'til Spitzer wanted to drop it and they dropped him instead."

Vail grudgingly allowed, "Had they left you the hell alone you'd have cleared up the simple misunderstanding about grazing fees sooner and them petty crooks would have still been in business. Where's the petty crook we're after now, and what in thunder has he done to deserve a four-man federal posse?"

Longarm said, "I told you that you didn't have to tag along, boss. Since you have, my aim is to nip a budding legend in the bud, alive, or apologize profusely if I've made a mistake. It happens, you know."

Vail growled, "I cut myself shaving all the time. Get to the goddamned point and quit trying for a trick ending, lest we all wind up confused if you get killed."

Longarm chuckled and said, "You got a point, and I can't stress it enough that we'd best take the notorious Kid Chinks alive so he can cringe his way to the gallows as an example to like-minded pool-hall pistoleers."

The normally long-winded Dutch, of all gents, snapped, "Damn it, Longarm . . ."

So Longarm nodded and said, "In the beginning I was up Durango way on another case. Knowing my rep and doubtless having heard I'm an easygoing cuss when halfway sober, Kid Chinks started up with me to impress his fellow bullyboys. When I thought it best to just leave than to spatter blood all over the interior of the Chapman Saloon, Kid Chinks bragged, and some believed, he'd backed a better known gunslick down."

"You should have shot him then and got it over with," said Smiley.

Longarm shrugged and said, "Be that as it may, I never. As a result of my common sense Kid Chinks maybe enjoyed a few rounds of drinks before it occurred to his big sister, Doris, if not yet to him, that a man with a rep, who can't really fight for shit, can be in a whole peck of trouble."

Old Dutch, a man with a rep who knew how to fight indeed, laughed unkindly and opined, "That accounts for them moving from Durango to Denver. But who beat his sister to death after she came to you for help?"

Longarm said, "Him, unless I'm making an awesome mistake. Neither child of the family had inherited brains worth mention, but she was a heap sweeter natured. She had this half-baked plan to get her kid brother off the hook. To him it must have looked as if she'd just commenced keeping serious company with the law. Like a fool I let her tag along with me as far as Thayer Junction and, like a fool, her riled-up brother followed."

Vail sighed and said, "Longarm, if I've told you once I've told you a hundred times not to play slap-and-tickle with female suspects!"

Longarm protested, "I never suspected Doris Drake of nothing but good will toward men, Billy. Getting back to my suspicions, the notorious but half-ass Kid Chinks tried to back-shoot me in Cheyenne and Thayer Junction. I winged him instead. So he stole the druggist's thoroughbred and lit out, leaving a trail even a white man could follow, so—"

"Back up. Who killed the gal?" asked Smiley, who trailed so good he might have found those parts less interesting.

Longarm said simply, "He could have beat his sister to death before or after he aimed at me so poorly. From the way the signs read up in our room I'd say he smacked her about before he'd been hurt too bad himself. I mean to ask him about that, as well as whether he meant to kill her or

179

just get her to tell him where I might best be back-shot.''

"Did she know?" asked Vail.

Longarm could only reply, "You know I never discuss my plans with females more than I feel I have to. With him demanding answers to things she didn't know, things could have gotten ugly, sudden. I think that must be them, down near the north end of this train.''

They could all see the half-dozen stockyard hands poking about in the dust and tricky sunset light amid the pole corrals and loading ramps ahead. As the four lawmen instinctively spread out a mite to approach in line abreast, Vail warned, "You're going to have to point your man out to us.''

Smiley growled, "Me and Dutch know him on sight, from scouting him out for Longarm. You can spot him best by his knee-length chaps and silver-mounted gun belt. Wears two fucking .45's to poke cows aboard freight trains. Ain't that a bitch?''

Longarm warned, "Let me worry about his guns. I want him alive. I mean that. I owe him a protracted trial as a kin killer if I'm right and, like I said, I could be wrong.''

"You keep saying that," growled Billy Vail. "I wish you'd make up your damned mind, old son. Are we after the silly shit or not?''

Longarm growled back, "I'll tell you the minute I get another good look at him in broad daylight. The first time we met, with him in the role of Kid Chinks, it was in a smoky saloon, and to tell the truth I'd had more than one drink. The second time we met, and that's only if we met a second time, he was behaving a heap nicer and sporting a full beard. I suspect he'd changed duds with a much taller man as well. The sheepherder's outfit he had on hung sort of shapeless and sloppy on him, now that I study back.''

Vail, having read as full a report on the whole affair as Longarm usually wired in, snapped his fingers and marveled, "Hot damn! I see which shell the pea went under, now! You winged the young shit in Thayer Junction. He stole a horse and lit out, with you trailing. Before you could catch up with him he came upon the real Shorty Blare, minding one of Kim Stover's herds. The sheepherder was likely as decent and lonesome as most gents alone on a desert. So he made the wounded fugitive welcome, and got shot down like a dog, along with his dog, who might have made a fuss about such wickedness.''

Longarm nodded and said, "All he had to do, then, was change or just partly change duds with the dead man, lash the corpse aboard the stolen horse, and run it off into the Tanglewaters. Everything after that went sort of automatic.''

"You're lucky he didn't back-shoot you when you rode in like a big-ass bird!'' said Dutch.

But Smiley growled, "Luck had nothing to do with it. The two-faced little shit must have been pissing his pants all the time he was flimflamming Longarm!''

By this time the cowpokes down the line had become aware of the four men short and tall moving in on them in step. They'd finished poking the last of the Denver beef aboard the Omaha-bound train. As they lined up abreast as thoughtfully, Vail muttered, "Oh, Lord, I hope nobody acts silly. How are you going to prove your grand notion even if that dead gal's kid brother and the young sheepherder you met later turn out to be the same cuss, old son?''

Longarm didn't answer. The train they were striding alongside had commenced to move north in a series of jerks as the engine took up the slack in all those couplers. Longarm had already busted into a run, having heard the steam-tweets way up the line. So as Vail bawled out, "Cut that out, you fool kid!'' Longarm simply hung on to a grab iron, running even faster, until he could hook a tie-rod with his left boot's instep and commence hauling himself up the barn-red corner of the rolling reefer.

As he got to the catwalk up above he saw that, sure enough, a distant figure wearing floppy chinked chaps was clinging to a brake wheel, hunkered down and, so far, not looking back.

Longarm started running along the catwalk and leaping from car top to car top as said cars rolled ever faster. The bends were still gentle as the tracks sort of bottlenecked together at the north end of the yards. But any turn at all at that speed tended to make a man feel he was about to be tossed off the train top. So Elroy Drake was hanging on for dear life and never looked up until Longarm, his own guts filled with fluttering bats, was almost on top of him.

As their eyes met, Longarm knew. Growing a thick short beard after the showdown in Durango and shaving it off after the flimflam on the Red Desert would only work when nobody was wondering whether or not he'd seen that common-featured face before. Longarm got his .44–40 out before Elroy could get up the nerve to let go the brake wheel. Longarm said, "I don't want to explain all this in Omaha, sonny. So we'd best get off here."

"How?" gasped the murderous but cowardly Kid Chinks, as the train rumbled on, ever faster, through the outskirts of town.

Longarm saw the longer they argued the faster the damned train would be going. So he kicked the young killer in the head, and as Kid Chinks sailed ass-over-tea-kettle backward off the train he just had to shove his gun back in its holster and jump.

He'd aimed to land on shortgrass where the tracks cut through a rise, affording a modest drop. When he wound up rolling and cussing farther than he'd have had to run for a base hit he sat up, spitting dust and dry grass stubble, to mutter, "Next time we'd best climb down the ladder a ways."

Then he rose and limped back along the now-cleared track to see how Kid Chinks had made out. As he did so he saw the tall Smiley and shorter Billy Vail and Dutch tearing up the track on a handcart.

182

He still beat them to where the youth he'd booted off the train lay moaning, tangled up in the coils of the wire fence that may have broken his fall but hadn't done him much other good.

As Longarm loomed over him Kid Chinks moaned, "You've busted my back, you bastard!" and then proved himself a liar by trying to get at the one six-gun he hadn't lost on his flight through time and space.

Longarm kicked him flat and told him, not unkindly, "You really ought to cut this buscadero bullshit out, Elroy. You just don't have what it takes to be bad as you'd like to be."

By this time Smiley and Dutch had pumped the handcart from the yards as close as they could. Billy Vail leaped as gracefully to earth as an older gent with a fat ass could and come down the bank to join Longarm and his battered prisoner, saying, "Well, I reckon him making a run for it as soon as he saw who was coming constitutes a sort of confession."

Longarm said, "I can do better, seeing his shirt's sort of tore already."

All three of them whistled when Longarm ripped out the front of the groggy gunslick's shirt to reveal the mustard plaster taped to the killer's rib cage. Vail said soberly, "If he's been treating his wound with a poltice all this time it means your bullet is still in him, as more evidence."

Longarm replied, "That's what I just said. Help me get this kin killer up aboard yon handcart and we'll make sure they treat him right at County General."

As Smiley and Dutch hunkered down to help Longarm disentangle the spiteful killer from the barbwire, Kid Chinks moaned, "Just leave me bleed to death in peace, damn your eyes! What sense does it make to nurse a poor boy back to health just so you can watch him hang in the end?"

Longarm told him, "Because you and me both owe it to Doris."

Kid Chinks said he didn't understand. The normally mo-

183

rose Smiley sounded almost cheerful as he replied, "Of course you don't understand. That's why they hang dumb sons of bitches like you more often than delicate young things like us."

Watch for

LONGARM AND THE CROOKED MARSHAL

138th novel in the bold LONGARM series
from Jove

Coming in June!

A special offer for people who enjoy reading the best Westerns published today. If you enjoyed this book, subscribe now and get ...

TWO FREE WESTERNS!
A $5.90 VALUE—NO OBLIGATION

If you enjoyed this book and would like to read more of the very best Westerns being published today, you'll want to subscribe to True Value's Western Home Subscription Service. If you enjoyed the book you just read and want more of the most exciting, adventurous, action packed Westerns, subscribe now.

TWO FREE BOOKS

When you subscribe, we'll send you your first month's shipment of the newest and best 6 Westerns for you to preview. With your first shipment, two of these books will be yours as our introductory gift to you absolutely FREE, regardless of what you decide to do.

Special Subscriber Savings

As a True Value subscriber all regular monthly selections will be billed at the low subscriber price of just $2.45 each. That's at least a savings of $3.00 each month below the publishers price. There is never any shipping, handling or other hidden charges. What's more there is no minimum number of books you must buy, you may return any selection for full credit and you can cancel your subscription at any time. A TRUE VALUE!

Mail the coupon below

To start your subscription and receive 2 FREE WESTERNS, fill out the coupon below and mail it today. We'll send you your first shipment which includes 2 FREE BOOKS as soon as we receive it.